"I'm hardly in a desperate state about the wedding being called off."

Wolf's tone of voice suggested he found the topic tiresome. "And that's because—" he continued.

"You didn't love her!" Cyn finished accusingly. "I already knew that. You're incapable of loving anyone! That's why I—" She broke off as she realized she'd been about to admit to having encouraged Rebecca to think very seriously before she committed herself to a marriage she wasn't sure of; that would be all the ammunition Wolf would need to rip her to pieces!

"Yes?" Wolf prompted, silkily soft.

Her cheeks were no longer pale now but darkly flushed. "Why *I* didn't marry you myself seven years ago!"

"All right, Cyn," he ground out harshly, a nerve pulsing in his rigidly clenched jaw, "I'll go. But if I ever find out you were instrumental in Rebecca's sudden flight, I'll—"

CAROLE MORTIMER, one of our most popular—and prolific—English authors, began writing in the Harlequin Presents series in 1979. She writes strong traditional romances with a distinctly modern appeal, and her winning way with characters and romantic plot twists has earned her an enthusiastic audience worldwide. Carole Mortimer lives on the Isle of Man with her family and menagerie of pets. She claims this busy household has helped to inspire her writing.

Books by Carole Mortimer

HARLEQUIN PRESENTS PLUS
1559—THE JILTED BRIDEGROOM
1583—PRIVATE LIVES
1607—MOTHER OF THE BRIDE
1631—ELUSIVE OBSESSION

HARLEQUIN PRESENTS
1258—ELUSIVE AS THE UNICORN
1325—A CHRISTMAS AFFAIR
1451—MEMORIES OF THE PAST
1468—ROMANCE OF A LIFETIME
1543—SAVING GRACE
1657—GRACIOUS LADY

Carole Mortimer

RETURN ENGAGEMENT

Harlequin Books

TORONTO • NEW YORK • LONDON
AMSTERDAM • PARIS • SYDNEY • HAMBURG
STOCKHOLM • ATHENS • TOKYO • MILAN
MADRID • WARSAW • BUDAPEST • AUCKLAND

For
Matthew Timothy Mortimer
I'm so proud you're
my son.

ISBN 0-373-11671-3

RETURN ENGAGEMENT

CHAPTER ONE

'Touches of *Lady Chatterley*, do you think?' Janie giggled.

Cyn made a slight acknowledging movement of the remark, although her attention was still held by the scene they were unwittingly witnessing.

They had been shown into this small reception-room only seconds ago by the rather haughty butler, while he left them to go off in search of Rebecca Harcourt, the young mistress of the house.

Cyn only hoped the young lady out in the garden wasn't her—otherwise their journey here could have been a wasted one!

She and Janie had driven into town especially to see the Harcourts, and had been suitably impressed by the house from the outside. The grounds the house stood in alone were almost as big as the park across which the house actually faced. Grand old houses like this one weren't so unusual in London, but the amount of ground attached to it was, Cyn was sure, given the expense of property in London and its immediate vicinity.

It was because of the size of the grounds that the Harcourts needed the gardener at all, she would say. And what a gardener—a tall golden god of a man, about twenty-five, his skin bronzed from the amount of time he obviously worked outside, although that colour was more likely to be simply weather-worn, considering it was only April and, what watery sun there was did not actually contain much heat just yet.

He had been working on one of the extensive borders outside when Cyn and Janie were shown into the reception-room, obviously absorbed in his work. He had seemed to remain so, when a young girl of about twenty crossed the landscaped lawn several feet away from him to enter the wooden-structure gazebo that stood in one corner of the garden facing away from the house. But seconds later he had straightened, glanced casually about him, before he too went into the gazebo.

Hence Janie's teasing remark! The girl who had crossed the garden, seemingly unaware of the gardener working there, hadn't looked like a maid, or anyone else who worked in the house for that matter. Her blaze of red hair was expertly styled, her make-up perfectly applied, the suit she was wearing designer-label, if Cyn wasn't mistaken.

God, she hoped it *wasn't* Rebecca Harcourt...! Because Cyn very much doubted that that Adonis of a gardener was her intended bridegroom.

Gerald Harcourt had actually been the one to make the appointment for Cyn to come here today, claiming his motherless daughter needed help organising her wedding, which was to take place in August. And organising weddings, and dealing with all the problems that seemed to bring along with it, was what Cyn did in her business, Perfect Bliss.

The idea for such a scheme had come to her out of the blue one day. Being stuck in yet another dead-end job, working for a particularly temperamental catering boss who often threw temper tantrums while they were actually working, was not what Cyn wanted to do with the rest of her life. The problem was, she didn't know what she did want to do either. She had gone through a long list of jobs the last few years—hotel receptionist, helper in a florist's, assistant in a bridal shop for a very short time too, all mixed up with waitressing jobs, plus training to be a printer at one stage, a job she knew she definitely wasn't cut out for after she had printed hundreds of posters inviting people to a Trafalgar Balls; her boss had been absolutely furious, and she could think of a few sailors who probably wouldn't have been too happy either! Needless to say, it had been a short-lived training.

Most of her jobs had been, but after a rather traumatic evening, where she had been helping her boss cater at a private dinner party in a gentleman's apartment, and his female guest had turned out to be the boss's own wife out for an evening of fun while her husband was working, Cyn had decided it was time for her and *that* particular job to part company. Especially when her boss had started throwing knives about the apartment; Cyn had decided there and then that he wasn't temperamental, just mental!

Unemployed again, she had sat down, briefly—she still had to pay the rent and the bills!—and thought over her career assets. Taken separately, they had seemed a bit haphazard, but when she put them all together...!

And so Perfect Bliss had emerged from the debris, the 'complete wedding' agency, designed to take away all the wear and tear—or did she mean tears?—from the bride and her family. Not that it had been an overnight success. After three years she still kept the agency ticking over with the occasional dinner party, but she had enough bookings for weddings not to take on too many other commitments. She had merely been waiting for the 'big one', as Janie called it, the society wedding that would get her name in those circles, where she hoped her agency might become fashionable once it was seen what a good job she did.

The Harcourt wedding was supposed to be that big break...!

Gerald Harcourt, a man in his early forties, had been a guest at one of the weddings Cyn had organised last weekend on Easter Saturday—a small affair in the country, and the bride was the daughter of a business friend, Gerald Harcourt had explained when he spoke to her during the wedding reception. He had been most impressed when he learnt that Cyn had organised the wedding, with the bride's requirements in mind, from the printing of the invitations to the perfect colour of the wedding bouquet—a bouquet *he* had somehow managed to catch when the bride threw it into the wedding crowd before departing on the honeymoon Cyn had also booked for the happy couple.

The bouquet disposed of, given to one of the bridesmaids accompanied by a charming smile, Gerald had questioned Cyn about Perfect Bliss, explaining that his own daughter, his only child, was being married later in the year, and, as his wife had died more than a dozen years ago, Rebecca was finding the whole thing rather a headache on her own. Cyn had been only too happy to talk to him as she helped clear away after the reception. She found his tall, distinguished looks, dark hair lightly sprinkled with grey at the temples, blue eyes warm in a face that was maturely handsome, his body still fit and lean in the dark three-piece suit he had worn for the wedding, more than passingly attractive. She found the idea of organising his daughter's wedding, the 'society wedding' she had been seeking, even *more* attractive, and she was more than willing to drive up from her little office in Feltham—she couldn't afford London rents on business property—to the Harcourt home and talk to the daughter in person at a time to be arranged once Gerald had spoken to Rebecca.

But if that girl in the garden *was* Rebecca Harcourt, Cyn had a feeling Gerald was going to be in for a nasty surprise concerning this wedding. Not to mention the bridegroom! Not that anyone had, so far. Like most grooms, he seemed to be remaining well out of the headache of organising the actual wedding.

Even as Cyn stood there watching, the gazebo door opened once again and the girl emerged, but from her distressed state she was obviously in floods of tears, giving one last anxious look in the direction of the gazebo before rushing across the garden towards the house.

Not a happy bride!

Cyn turned away with a sigh, more than ever convinced that her journey here today had been a wasted one. If—— She looked across the room as the door opened to admit, not Rebecca Harcourt, but Gerald himself.

'My dear Cyn!' he greeted her warmly, giving her one of his welcoming smiles. He was dressed in a dark business suit today and looking very lean and handsome. 'I'm so sorry you've been kept waiting,' he said regretfully as he crossed the room to her side, 'but we seem to be having a little difficulty locating Rebecca.' This last was added with a frown.

Cyn knocked Janie's arm as she sensed that her young assistant had been about to blab Rebecca's presence in the garden; unless she was very much mistaken, Rebecca Harcourt wouldn't want her father to know she had been anywhere near the garden—or the young and handsome gardener! She might be wrong, of course, but somehow she doubted it.

'That's perfectly all right,' she returned smoothly. 'We were just admiring your home.' In fact, she hadn't taken too much notice of it since they had come inside and she had seen the formal elegance of the rooms, the antique furniture, the original paintings on the walls; all the trappings of wealth that people like the Harcourts took so much for granted. It was all very nice, but it wasn't for Cyn.

Gerald looked pleased by her comment, looking about him appreciatively. He was obviously a man who enjoyed what his wealth could give him. 'We like it,' he dismissed. 'Did you—— ?'

'Aren't you going to introduce us, Gerald?' interrupted a silkily soft voice.

A voice Cyn instantly recognised!

But it couldn't be. Not here. *Why* here? came her next unbidden question, as she knew she *wasn't* mistaken, that she would know that voice anywhere.

Wolf Thornton's voice...

She couldn't move. She did try, but not one single muscle in her body seemed to be obeying her at the moment. Her feet felt like lead weights rooted to the carpeted floor, her body so still and tense that she might have been a statue. She knew her face was as pale as alabaster, so she might almost have been one!

Her head was held at a taut angle, her eyes riveted to a spot above the fireplace, and she tried to remember what she was wearing today. *What she was wearing?* What difference did that make? Wolf Thornton was standing somewhere behind her, and she doubted if he was going to be any more pleased to see her than she was to see him.

Would he have changed? Had she? It was seven years since she had last seen him; of course she had changed!

Her hair was no longer that cascade of moonlight silver-blond it had been when she was twenty, but styled to her shoulders in a feathered cut that was easier to manage, and the violet-blue eyes were no longer so naïve and unaware. Her even features were the same, of course—the slightly too short nose, the wide smiling mouth, the small pointed chin that could still lift defensively. And she still wore some of the clothes she had owned seven years ago. She couldn't afford to replace them, so she knew she hadn't put on any weight! *Did* Wolf still look the same? She was still too stunned to be able to turn and look—too frightened of what she would see in his face, too, when he saw it was her!

'Glad you could make it,' Gerald was greeting the other man now. 'I've only just got in from the office myself. Although it's just as well we decided to meet here after all; Rebecca seems to have done one of her disappearing acts again,' he added indulgently.

'She'll turn up,' the other man dismissed smoothly. 'She always does.'

Oh, God, that voice. Cyn shivered in reaction, feeling waves of sheer terror coursing through her now. The last time she had seen Wolf Thornton she had made it perfectly clear exactly what she thought of him, and she had no reason to believe that the intervening years—she had had no contact with him during that time—had done anything to soften *his* feelings towards her.

How could this be happening to her? Of course, Wolf ran Thornton Industries, and Gerald Harcourt ran his own company, which was just as powerfully successful; so why *shouldn't* the two businessmen be friends? But why had the two men had to meet today, and here of all places?

She could see Janie looking at her curiously now—when the girl could tear her gaze away from the man standing over by the door, that was! Wolf still had that animal magnetism that was so attractive to women, Cyn saw with dismay.

It was that realisation that finally broke the spell for her; Wolf always had been able to draw the women to him, and it had been something he took full advantage of.

She turned determinedly, that pointed chin at a defensive angle, her breath catching in her throat as she looked at Wolf for the first time in seven years. He *hadn't* changed; that dark blond hair was still too long to be fashionable, several straight tendrils falling over his forehead, his golden-brown eyes surrounded by the longest dark lashes Cyn had ever seen on a man or a woman, his nose long and straight, his mouth—— His mouth *wasn't* the same, she realised with a frown. In the past his mouth had been a sensual invitation, the lower lip fuller than the top one, but now it was a thin slash of cynicism, looking as if he rarely smiled, the lines beside his nose and mouth not caused by laughter but by a harshness that seemed to underline all his features, Cyn realised as she looked closer at him, his eyes not a warm golden-brown at all, but as hard and unyielding as the gold they resembled.

And they became harder still as he seemed to sense her gaze on him and looked across at her, an instant flare of recognition in his expression, his mouth thinning even more as his jaw tightened, his eyes narrowed to steely slits as he straightened challengingly. Whereas in the past he had seemed possessed of a timeless quality, a natural enthusiasm that made it difficult to pinpoint his age, today he looked every one of his thirty-five years.

Cyn swallowed hard. She had never felt more like fleeing in her life before—fleeing *for* her life! There had been a time in her life when she feared Wolf *might* actually kill her.

'Gerald——?' Wolf's control never wavered as he turned pointedly to the other man, still obviously waiting for that introduction.

As if he didn't know exactly who she was! She refused to believe he had forgotten her. He might have wished he could, but she knew from his reaction a moment ago, when he first looked at her, that he certainly hadn't.

'Sorry, Wolf,' the older man smiled easily, completely unaware of any tension in the room. 'This is Lucynda Smith, of Perfect Bliss,' he explained lightly. 'Although it's Cyn to her friends, she assures me,' he added teasingly.

Wolf didn't look as if he found anything in the least amusing about her name, or her! And the speculative look he gave the other man seemed to question just how much of a 'friend' of hers Gerald considered himself to be.

It was an interesting question; as well as asking Cyn to call here when they had spoken on Saturday, Gerald had also invited her out to dinner. The first she had been only too happy to organise, the latter she had said they would talk about further when they met again. She hadn't envisaged Wolf Thornton also being present when that happened. In fact, she had always pushed firmly from her mind any thoughts that she and Wolf would *ever* meet again!

'And this is my assistant, Janie Harrison,' she put in firmly.

Janie looked grateful for the recognition, although for all the notice Wolf took of her Cyn might as well have saved her breath—although Gerald, charmingly polite as ever, acknowledged the girl with a welcoming smile. Janie blushed furiously. Her hair was not the rich auburn of Rebecca Harcourt but that ginger-blond that usually accompanied excessively pale skin. Poor Janie looked much younger than her eighteen years in her girlish pleasure at being in the company of two such presentable men.

Wolf Thornton wasn't *presentable*, Cyn thought slightly resentfully; his ignoring of Janie, in order to continue looking at *her* with that chilling intensity, bordered on rudeness. Not that Janie looked too concerned; she was obviously as much in awe of this man, who looked so much like his name implied—fierce and untameable!—as she was attracted to him!

'*Miss* Smith?' Wolf said softly in answer to Gerald's introduction.

Colour warmed her cheeks at his unspoken implication. She knew to what he was referring, of course; the last time they had met it had looked as if she was about to marry Roger Collins.

'A case of "always the bridesmaid, never the bride," I'm afraid,' she returned lightly, meeting his gaze with an effort now.

Why was he continuing to behave as if the two of them had never met before? Why didn't he just tell Gerald Harcourt that he knew exactly what her friends called her—her enemies too?

If he was surprised at her never having been married after all, then he didn't show it. 'Then forgive me for asking,' he rasped in a completely unapologetic voice. 'But if that's the case, by what experience do you claim to be able to organise other brides' weddings for them, especially one like Rebecca's?'

He was meaning to be insulting—and he succeeded! He knew very well about her own working-class background, the distaste she had for so-called 'society', and he was taunting her with that knowledge.

'Oh, come on, Wolf,' Gerald dismissed lightly, still unaware of the undercurrents to the conversation taking place between Cyn and Wolf. 'You don't have to have been knocked over by a bus to know what the consequences will be. In my mind there isn't much difference between getting married and being run over,' he explained with a rueful grimace as everyone turned to look at him because of the simile he had used. 'Both knock you off your feet and leave you completely disorientated!'

'I hope none of my brides ever gets to talk to you on the subject.' Cyn shook her head, unable to hold back a smile. 'Otherwise I'd be out of a job!'

'Talking of that job...' Gerald frowned now. 'I'll go and have another look for Rebecca,' he told them absently before leaving the room.

Cyn had never been so grateful for Janie's pleading to come with her that morning than she was at this moment. Otherwise she would have been left alone in the room with Wolf. And by the time Gerald returned the room could have been reduced to bloody carnage. No, that was an exaggeration. Wolf didn't look as if he had ever needed to be physically violent; he could probably fatally wound with the rapier-sharpness of his tongue when crossed, reduce an adversary to a quaking mass with the coldness of his gaze.

The silence that descended on the room after Gerald's departure was oppressive—or was it only Cyn who saw it that way? She chanced a glance at Wolf and saw he was still watching her with those coldly narrowed eyes, and quickly looked away again. Janie, sweet, kind Janie, who could calm the mother of the bride with so little fuss it was hardly noticeable that there had ever been anything to calm, was gazing at Wolf with an infatuated glow in her pale green eyes.

Cyn felt angry on her behalf for the way in which Wolf didn't even acknowledge that adoration, even though he must be aware of it: Janie was a little too obvious for him not to be! No doubt he was used to having girls finding him attractive, but that was no reason for him to be so damned blasé about it!

She wasn't used to seeing him quite so formally dressed as he was today. His dark three-piece suit and snowy white shirt were austere in their impeccable tailoring; a grey silk tie was knotted severely at his throat. He wore no jewellery; he had always deplored the use of it by men, and his only adornment was a plain gold watch strapped to his left wrist above one long sensitive hand. His hands, Cyn saw with a fascination of her own, were just the same, long and artistic, nevertheless as strong as a vice when they needed to be, the nails kept deliberately short.

Wolfram James Thornton. She had expected to hear more of the name over the last seven years, but the only thing she had heard it used in connection with was Thornton Industries. The business section of the newspapers often carried articles about the rapidly expanding company; it seemed the family business had prospered under his guidance. Strange, she had never thought of Wolf as a businessman. But then seven years ago he hadn't been . . .

'So—Cyn, wasn't it?' he drawled hardly, challengingly, 'you're going to wave your magic wand and make this wedding perfect for Rebecca?'

Her cheeks felt warm at the insult behind his taunt. 'I hope so, yes,' she confirmed tautly.

He strode further into the room, at once dominating the intimacy of his surroundings. 'A flowing white gown, a cake with little cupids decorating it, a horse and carriage to drive the bride and groom from the church to the wedding reception?'

Cyn paled as he used his words like sharp barbs to wound her; he hadn't forgotten a thing! She drew in a shaky breath. 'The latter might be a little difficult to organise in the middle of London,' she dismissed sharply, her hands clenched so tightly she could feel her nails digging into her palms.

'I'm sure it could be arranged—if that's what the bride would really like,' Wolf returned harshly.

She swallowed hard, deliberately turning away from the cold implacability of his face to look at Janie. 'I seem to have forgotten to bring my notebook in with me—do you think you could go out to the van and get it for me?' she requested warmly—the notebook in question feeling as if it were burning a hole through her handbag into her hip as she told the lie!

But this barbed conversation with Wolf, of which no one else seemed aware, just couldn't continue. Much as she hated the idea, if he was a very good friend of the Harcourt family, a frequent visitor to the house, maybe she should just withdraw from being involved in this wedding at all. She could save herself an awful lot of work if she established that fact right now!

'Of course,' Janie agreed readily, shooting Wolf a longing look as she sidled past him and then out of the door.

'Well... Cyn-to-your-friends,' Wolf grated contemptuously as soon as they were alone, his golden gaze

raking over her with slow insult, 'just how long have
you been a "friend" of Gerald's?'

She drew in a sharp breath at the deliberate provo-
cation of the remark. 'I——'

'It can't have been for very long,' Wolf added scathingly. 'He only dropped his last mistress a matter of
weeks ago.'

'I'm not his mistress!' Cyn hissed the denial, wondering if these heated spots of colour—through anger
this time—were going to remain a fixture in her cheeks
while she spoke to this hateful man. 'We only met for
the first time on Saturday!'

Wolf's mouth twisted derisively, those lines grooved
into his cheeks intensifying. 'No, possibly you can't be
classed as a mistress yet; give it another few weeks or
so! But don't give yourself any false hopes where he's
concerned; you heard Gerald's views on marriage,' he
added harshly.

She gave a weary sigh. 'I don't have any "false hopes",
or indeed hopes of any other kind, where Gerald
Harcourt is concerned; I barely know the man.' She
shook her head dismissively.

'It's obvious he has more in mind than just a business
arrangement between the two of you,' Wolf rasped
coldly, his eyes narrowed speculatively.

Taking into account that initial dinner invitation she
had received from Gerald, he was no doubt right. But
even if he was, it was none of his business if she and
Gerald Harcourt should choose to go out together. Or
if, indeed, they should become lovers. Just because he
was a friend of Gerald's, there was no reason for
him——

'It will never happen, Cyn,' Wolf told her softly, his sharp gaze easily able to read her resentful thoughts. 'Believe me.'

Her head went back challengingly—rather like a kitten putting itself up against a wolf! Wolf was tall and masculine, well over six feet in height, whereas she was barely five feet in her bare feet, not much more than that in the flat shoes she wore with black tailored trousers and matching jacket, the purple blouse she wore beneath the jacket making her eyes look almost the same colour. She looked tiny and slender, nothing like the twenty-seven she actually was—and this man was trying to intimidate her. Well, he wasn't going to succeed!

'My relationship—or otherwise—with Gerald is none of your concern,' she told him waspishly, her eyes flashing.

'I would make it so, Cyn,' he assured her softly, warningly.

She frowned across at him, that frown deepening at the stark bitterness in that harshly hewn face. 'You have no right, Wolf,' she choked. 'No right at all!'

'I have every right, damn you!' he began fiercely, his eyes glittering deeply gold as he took a threatening step towards her. 'You——'

'I couldn't find it, Cyn,' a slightly breathless Janie came back into the room at that moment, her face slightly flushed from her exertions. 'I looked in the back of the van as well as the front and I——'

'I found the notebook, Janie,' Cyn told her guiltily, knowing she had wasted Janie's time, as well as her own, trying to talk to Wolf alone in these circumstances; the differences between Wolf and herself were too deeply embedded to be dealt with in a few minutes of private conversation between them. 'I realised it was in my bag after all almost as soon as you'd left the room, but by that time it was too late to stop you. I'm sorry about that,' she smiled apologetically at the other girl, although to her credit, Janie didn't look in the least put out; she was preoccupied once again gazing up enchanted at Wolf!

And he was looking at Cyn with such a look of intense dislike that a shiver of apprehension ran the length of her spine. They might not have resolved anything by their conversation just now, the intensity of his gaze seemed to say, but then the conversation was far from over. Oh, God!

Cyn turned gratefully towards the door as it opened to readmit Gerald, closely followed by the errant Rebecca. Cyn's relief turned to dismay as she realised it *was* the girl from the garden...

All signs of recent tears had been completely erased by the subtle use of make-up. Rebecca Harcourt was even more beautiful close to like this, her skin flawless, her features smooth and even. And if there was a lingering anxiety in the deep blue of her eyes, Cyn felt sure she was the only one aware of it.

'I'm so sorry I kept you waiting.' Rebecca's voice was huskily low—from those recent tears, or naturally so, Cyn couldn't be sure. 'I didn't realise you were here,' she added awkwardly.

But, to Cyn's puzzlement, the remarks weren't being made to her. Rebecca was looking up at Wolf as she crossed the room to his side.

'Hello, darling.' Rebecca reached up to kiss him lightly on the lips. 'I'm so glad you could get away from the office so we could both talk to Miss Smith about the arrangements for the wedding.' Now she turned towards Cyn, smiling a welcome.

Cyn just stared. She couldn't have made a response even if she had wanted to. *Wolf* was Rebecca's bridegroom...?

'You know, I suddenly realised after I'd gone off in search of Rebecca,' Gerald spoke ruefully, 'that I never did get around to introducing Wolf to you, Cyn.' He squeezed her arm apologetically for his oversight. 'This is Wolf Thornton, my daughter's fiancé.'

Wolf *was* the bridegroom!

CHAPTER TWO

'SOME people have all the luck,' Janie sighed at Cyn's side as they made the drive back to the office a short time later.

'Hmm?' Cyn answered distractedly, still too shaken to even try to guess to what Janie was alluding; she had just spent almost an hour going through what arrangements the 'happy couple' would like for their August wedding, with Wolf being as objectionable as he could be without making it look like yet another personal attack on her. Or perhaps he was always like that nowadays? She hadn't thought of that.

'Rebecca Thornton,' Janie enlightened her with another sigh. 'It doesn't seem fair that she has a gorgeous father like that and a sexy fiancé most women would kill for!'

Cyn couldn't help her half-smile. 'I don't think having a good-looking father counts,' she said ruefully.

'Perhaps not,' the other girl conceded with a dismissive shrug. 'But Wolf Thornton is something else!'

Oh, he was 'something else' all right, Cyn acknowledged inwardly; although exactly what he was, she wasn't about to regale Janie with!

'I wonder where the gardener fits into all this?' Janie added thoughtfully.

Cyn sobered; she had been wondering the same thing. They certainly hadn't imagined the intensity of the encounter between Rebecca and the young gardener, on Rebecca's part at least; they hadn't actually seen the young man emerge from the gazebo, Gerald's arrival in the small sitting-room distracting their attention from the garden at that moment. But it was safe to assume, from the little they had seen, that the gardener did 'fit in' somewhere!

If it had been anyone else but Wolf who was the bridegroom in this job, Cyn probably wouldn't have given it another thought; after all, it was none of her business whom the bride chose to meet, in the open or otherwise. All that concerned her was that the bride turned up on the wedding-day, and that all the arrangements ran as smoothly as they were supposed to. But the bridegroom *was* Wolf——

God, she could still hardly believe that! Rebecca was twenty at a guess—younger, not older, if anything, and Wolf was already thirty-five, a mature, experienced thirty-five at that; why on earth was he marrying a girl almost young enough to be his daughter? More to the point, why was Rebecca marrying him, when at the same time she was having assignations with young gardeners at her father's home! Cyn didn't doubt that Wolf would be furiously angry if he should ever find out about that. Not that she, for one, intended telling him, but perhaps Rebecca should . . . ?

She had watched the engaged couple when she didn't think she was being observed herself; they seemed to get on well enough, although hardly in a lover-like way, Wolf treating Rebecca with the same indulgence her father did, Rebecca slightly in awe of him as she deferred to him over every decision. Even over where she should buy her wedding-dress! Cyn certainly wouldn't have consulted him——

What was she thinking of? This was Rebecca's marriage to Wolf, a relationship she could already see was in serious trouble. Although perhaps not. How did she know what arrangement Rebecca and Wolf had for after their wedding? Wolf was a stranger to her now, bearing little resemblance to the man she had known—thought she had known?—seven years ago, so perhaps he and Rebecca were going to have the sort of relationship where they *both* had other friends, lovers, as well as each other.

It was somehow a depressing thought to have about a marriage that hadn't even begun yet.

Whatever, the last hour had been one of the most traumatic of Cyn's life. She had been constantly on edge in case Wolf should finally say something that would reveal to the Harcourts that the two of them had met before, which would be very embarrassing when they had behaved like strangers from the outset. Embarrassing for Wolf too, but, as she knew from experience, he didn't give a damn what people thought of him, and it would be a way of scoring off her.

And the longer the meeting carried on, without him saying something, the more tense and agitated Cyn had become. Especially as Wolf had seemed to become more and more relaxed as he obviously—to her—enjoyed her growing discomfort, that golden-brown gaze never far from her flushed face. Damn him!

And as she and Janie had taken their leave, she had known from Wolf's expression that this wasn't the last she was going to see of him for another seven years, that, whatever the outcome of this wedding, he would make sure of that!

'Perhaps he doesn't fit in at all.' Janie gave a dismissive shrug at Cyn's lack of a verbal response. 'After all, what woman in her right mind would even look at another man when she was going to marry someone like Wolf Thornton?'

Cyn gave a pained wince; what woman, indeed! How naïve poor Janie still was at eighteen; she hadn't yet realised that there was much more to choosing a life's partner than the way he looked. But the important question was, had Rebecca Harcourt realised it, now that it was almost too late and she was due to marry in a few months' time? Almost...? It *was* too late, with Wolf as the bridegroom!

She determinedly put the Harcourt-Thornton wedding from her mind once they got back to the office; she had a business to run, and she wouldn't be able to do that effectively if she allowed herself to think of Wolf. She had spent seven years not thinking about him, and, while it hadn't always been easy, she had somehow managed to get on with her life. He had no right disrupting things for her in this way when she was on the brink of finally making a breakthrough with her business. The unfortunate factor was that Wolf's wedding to Rebecca Harcourt was going to be instrumental in helping her achieve that breakthrough!

She picked the receiver up automatically when the telephone rang a short time after their return, although she immediately tensed when the caller identified herself as Rebecca Harcourt.

'What can I do for you, Miss Harcourt?' she enquired with polite distance. She usually made a point of getting on friendly terms with all the brides she dealt with. She had found from experience that it made things better all round if the two of them could talk easily together, but that wasn't going to be easy for her with this girl, not when Wolf was the man Rebecca intended marrying!

'Rebecca, please,' the girl requested a little breathlessly. 'And what you can do for me is—well——'

'Yes?' Cyn prompted when she realised Rebecca seemed to be having difficulty finishing what she wanted to say. 'If it's that you've decided you don't want to use my agency after all, please don't worry that I'll be offended,' she added lightly—in the circumstances, she would be relieved if this turned out to be the case! 'I realise that perhaps your father put you in a position where——'

'Oh, it isn't that,' Rebecca hastened to reassure her. 'I'm sure that your help with things is going to be invaluable,' she accepted distractedly. 'I just——' She broke off awkwardly.

'Yes?' Cyn urged again, more gently this time, sensing the girl's strain. And what was the point of her being distant with Rebecca? It wasn't the girl's fault that she was marrying Wolf, of all people!

'I—— Could you——?'

Oh, dear! Cyn had a feeling that the meeting Rebecca had had with the gardener in the gazebo was going to be important after all!

'Everything's going too fast.' Rebecca finally seemed to find the right words, sounding relieved as she did. 'I'm sure I'm not the first bride you've found to have a touch of pre-wedding nerves,' she attempted to dismiss lightly. 'I just—well, I want you to slow down on the arrangements for a bit,' she added brightly, obviously feeling more confident now. 'There's no rush, and——'

'The wedding date is only four months away,' Cyn reminded her quietly.

'Well, yes. But—— Well——'

'How about if just the two of us got together for a chat?' Cyn took pity on her. As Rebecca said, she was accustomed to dealing with last-minute jitters, but four

months away could hardly be called 'last-minute.'
Besides, she had a feeling this was so much more serious
than that.

'Oh, yes,' Rebecca agreed gratefully. 'That would be
marvellous. I could—try to explain, then.'

Cyn doubted that very much. She had a feeling
Rebecca was trying to deny the truth even to herself.
'How about if I come back to the house tomorrow, and
we can——?'

'Oh, not here!' Rebecca cut in sharply. 'What I mean
is,' she forced her voice to sound lightly dismissive, 'why
don't we have lunch together somewhere, at least make
the meeting enjoyable?'

And as far away from her father and Wolf as possible,
Cyn would hazard a guess. 'That's fine with me,' she
accepted. 'How about——?' She broke off abruptly as
her office door swung open without warning, staring up
at Wolf as he stood so arrogantly in the doorway. Her
hand tightened instinctively round the telephone receiver, the colour draining from her cheeks even as she
felt her mouth go dry.

Although why she was so disconcerted she didn't
know. She had known earlier that there was no way Wolf
was meekly going to accept her reappearance into his
life, after an absence of seven years, without making her
well aware of his displeasure, for all that he had remained so outwardly calm while they were both still at
the Harcourts'. Meekly? Wolf had never accepted anything meekly in his life!

No, what was making this second meeting with him
in one day so awkward for Cyn was that, for all the
other girl's bravado as to her reason for calling, Cyn
could almost guarantee that Wolf was the last person
Rebecca would want to know about this telephone call.

And as they were still connected, and Cyn had no way of letting the other girl know of her fiancé's arrival without at the same time alerting Wolf to the identity of the person on the other end of the line, Cyn wasn't quite sure what to do next!

She watched Wolf as he came fully into the office, closing the door firmly behind him, standing across the room to look at her with haughty disdain as he waited for her to end the call. As end it she surely must. And as quickly as possible.

'Lunch sounds fine,' she somehow managed to answer Rebecca, although she could hear the strain in her own voice as she tried to sound normal. 'Perhaps you could name a restaurant that would be convenient for both of us?' she added lightly, all the time watching Wolf as he moved about the office now, occasionally picking things up to examine them before discarding them again, as if he had had no real interest in them in the first place. As, indeed, he probably hadn't. She had bridal books, printers' books, schedules, all littered about the gaily decorated office, its pink and cream wallpaper and paint applied by Cyn herself; she hadn't been able to afford to pay a professional after putting down her first years' rent on the office itself! The disdainful twist of Wolf's harshly etched lips seemed to say he was well aware of the amateurish attempt she had made at decorating. He turned back to her now, dark blond brows raised pointedly as she still remained on the telephone.

Cyn would gladly end the call, if Rebecca would just name a restaurant. The sooner she got this meeting with Wolf over and done with the better. And after it, her meeting with Rebecca would probably be superfluous anyway: Wolf hadn't said so at the time, but Cyn was sure she was the last person he wanted involved in the organisation of his wedding to Rebecca.

Thank goodness Janie had gone out for a late lunch on their return, otherwise her assistant would have been agog with curiosity as to the reason for Wolf Thornton calling on Cyn here after they had so recently spoken at his fiancé's house. Cyn certainly had no intention of explaining to the girl that there were certain things Wolf would like to say to her that he wouldn't want anyone else to be witness to!

'How about the Ritz?' Rebecca finally suggested after what seemed to Cyn like an extraordinarily long time. It probably wasn't, but with Wolf still prowling around the room, it certainly seemed that way!

And the Ritz was hardly 'convenient to both of them,' or indeed within Cyn's budget, but as this was to be a business meeting it would have to go on expenses; she certainly couldn't waste the time—or, indeed, give away Rebecca's identity—by suggesting somewhere else.

'Fine,' she accepted tersely. 'Twelve-thirty to-morrow,' she ended the call, putting the receiver down abruptly before turning to look at Wolf where he had moved around behind her now, studying the wall-chart she had of future bookings for the services of Perfect Bliss. Several dinner parties were also booked down during the more barren weeks.

He turned to her abruptly now, his golden-brown gaze rapier-sharp as it raked over her contemptuously, making Cyn very aware of the slightly windswept appearance of her silver-blond hair as it fell in soft waves to her shoulders, the colour made to look even lighter against the dark violet of her blouse. Her lips, she knew, would be bare of lip-gloss too, as she had just drunk the mug of coffee she had made to tide herself over until she went out for her own lunch once Janie returned.

This wasn't how she had wanted to see Wolf again, but then she hadn't been expecting to see him again so soon. She should have remembered that Wolf always did the unexpected.

Her jaw rose defensively as she deliberately met the cold disdain of his gaze. 'What are you doing here, Wolf?' she challenged, her voice—thank goodness—not showing by so much as a quiver how much his presence here unnerved her. And unnerve her it did. The two of them were completely alone here, with not much chance of an early reprieve for Cyn.

His mouth twisted, accentuating those deep grooves in his cheeks. 'You surely didn't think our conversation was over?' he drawled derisively, giving her a pitying look now for her naïveté.

She drew in a ragged breath. 'Which conversation would that be, Wolf?' She arched blond brows questioningly. 'The one from this morning—or the one from seven years ago?'

If she had thought he looked harshly remote before then now he looked positively icy, his eyes hard gold orbs, his mouth a thin slash of anger, his jaw clenched at an aggressive angle.

'The two are surely connected?' he bit out through clenched teeth, as if it was taking every effort of will on his part to stop himself from physically hauling her out of the chair, lifting her completely off her feet, and shaking her until her teeth rattled.

Cyn forced herself to remain seated, when what she really wanted to do was jump out of the chair and run, just run and run, until she was sure this man couldn't catch her. But as she knew from experience, if Wolf really wanted to catch up with someone then he would.

So instead of running she gave a dismissive movement of her head. 'I don't see how,' she shrugged, her fingers white as she held tightly on to the pen she had been using to work with when Rebecca's call came in.

Wolf's eyes narrowed on the pale defiance of her face. 'Was that Gerald on the phone just now, arranging to have lunch with you tomorrow?'

The change of subject was so totally unexpected that for a moment Cyn was taken aback at the sudden twist, then a resentful flush darkened her cheeks. 'Whether it was or it wasn't is none of your business, Wolf,' she told him as she finally stood up—not that it gave her much of an advantage, as Wolf still overshadowed her by more than a foot. But at least she was mobile now if the need to run should become a necessity! 'I can have lunch with whoever I damn well please,' she added defiantly. She was sure it wouldn't even occur to him that it was *Rebecca* Harcourt who had arranged to meet her for lunch tomorrow. And she had no intention of telling him that little fact either!

One of his hands moved so fast that Cyn was barely aware of the movement, although she couldn't mistake his grasp on her wrist as his long fingers curled about her tender flesh like steel bands. Just as she couldn't mistake the warm flush that suddenly emanated through her body at the touch of those long tapered fingers, which she knew could caress with such tenderness, move over the soft curves of her body with such——

No! She hadn't thought about Wolf in that way for seven years, hadn't allowed herself that luxury, and to do so now, when he was about to marry another woman, was sheer madness!

'Let go of me, Wolf,' she instructed tautly, unable to look into the dark tormented beauty of his face, staring down at the spot where his flesh touched hers, his hand so dark against her much paler skin.

Again long-denied memories came flooding back to pain her, and, with a strength she hadn't known she was capable of, she wrenched her arm out of his grasp, the pain this caused her a physical one rather than an emotional one. And she could deal with the physical pain so much more easily than the emotional one this man had once inflicted on her; she knew that the bruises on her skin would fade, that the inner ones never would.

'How is your family, Wolf?' she asked with disdain, her expression one of challenge.

His eyes glazed over coldly. 'Family?' he repeated, dangerously soft. 'There's only my mother and Barbara now.'

Only his mother and Barbara? There didn't need to be anyone else; the pair were formidable enough on their own!

Cyn gave an acknowledging inclination of her head. 'And how are they?'

His mouth twisted. 'Do you really care?'

No, she didn't care in the least, but at least the mention of the two of them had diverted his attention away from the source of that telephone call he had just interrupted. 'No,' she answered truthfully, unflinching as the dangerous glitter deepened in his eyes, remembering all too well the dislike the other two women had for her, and the way, in the past, they had never lost an opportunity to show that dislike. She was sure they would be no more interested in her well-being now than she was in theirs! Although, to be fair, it had always been Claudia Thornton who had disapproved of her the most, being totally against her son's relationship with Cyn. Barbara had represented a different sort of threat completely.... Did she still? If she did, then Cyn had more reason to pity Rebecca than she had originally thought.

'I didn't think so,' Wolf rasped now, the suppressed anger in his body a tangible thing, his very stillness unsettling.

Cyn gave a weary sigh. 'What do you want here, Wolf? Rehashing the past isn't going to help anyone. It's your future you should be concentrating on,' she added with a frown, her thoughts once again on the strange behaviour of Rebecca Harcourt this morning, and the even more enigmatic telephone call she had received from the other girl a short time ago.

Wolf was watching her closely, that amber gaze narrowed coldly. 'And just what do you mean by that?' he finally prompted softly.

Cyn had no intention of betraying Rebecca, and shrugged dismissively. 'Do you love Rebecca Harcourt?'

He drew in a harsh breath. 'What the hell do my feelings for Rebecca have to do with you?'

A lot more than any friendship she might have with Gerald Harcourt had to do with him! Wolf seemed to think he could walk back into her life after seven years, albeit unknowingly, and demand all sorts of things from her, but she wasn't to be allowed the same privilege where *he* was concerned!

'Feelings, Wolf?' she scoffed with derision. 'I don't believe you have any for Rebecca.' She shook her head. 'At least, not the sort of feelings you should have towards the woman you intend making your wife,' she frowned.

Wolf moved now, crossing the room with soundless footsteps, to stand only inches in front of her, his very proximity intimidating—as it was meant to be. 'And what would you know about that, Cyn?' he scorned forcefully. 'What the hell did you ever know—or care!—about the way I felt?'

That was unfair—totally unfair. For a few weeks, a few precious weeks that had affected the rest of Cyn's life, she had thought she knew this man—and his emotions—very well. The fact that that belief had been proved incorrect couldn't take that away from her. And she was sure—dammit, she *knew*—that Wolf wasn't in love with Rebecca! So why was he marrying her? Why had he never married Barbara, as she had thought he eventually would?

Cyn looked up at Wolf now, a sheen of tears blurring her vision of him, blunting all the sharp edges and angles to his face, briefly giving him the appearance of the man she had known all those years ago, a man who, although confident of himself and his own abilities, certainly hadn't been possessed of the hard arrogance this almost-stranger portrayed.

And then she blinked, erasing the tears—and that erroneous impression of Wolf being at all the approachable man she had once known. Before her stood a man whose face was lined with bitterness, a sharp dissatisfaction about the thin line of his once sensual mouth, his eyes no longer like liquid gold but hard and unyielding. Perhaps he had always been this way, and she had just been too infatuated to realise?

No! She couldn't, wouldn't, believe that, because that would make a mockery of all she had once felt for him. And it had been so important in her life.

She drew herself up defensively. 'We aren't discussing me, Wolf,' she told him briskly. 'Why are you marrying Rebecca?' She looked at him intently.

His mouth twisted, his hands thrust into his trouser pockets now, his suit jacket pushed back carelessly, revealing the flatness of his stomach beneath the fitted waistcoat. Wolf had always been slim, but now he was whipcord so, muscles rippling beneath taut skin. 'Why do you think I'm marrying her?' he returned softly, his mouth twisted mockingly.

Cyn was about to dismiss her right to 'think' anything about his relationship with Rebecca, and then she stopped, remembering Wolf's easy familiarity with Gerald Harcourt, the obvious friendship between the two men. And she knew *exactly* why Wolf was marrying the young girl, and also why Rebecca had agreed to marry him.

'A business arrangement,' she said with obvious disgust. 'My God, Wolf,' she looked at him pityingly, 'what happened to you?' She shook her head dazedly.

His eyes were icy slits. 'Happened to me?' he repeated with cold menace.

Cyn stared at him as if she had never seen him before—as, indeed, she was sure she never had known this man. 'Is this what you've become, Wolf, a hard-nosed businessman like Alex——?'

'Leave Alex out of this!' Wolf cut in harshly, no longer relaxed, his hands clenched into fists at his sides now. 'He's dead.'

She knew his brother was dead, had still been in Wolf's life when the helicopter Alex had liked to fly himself, to get him to and from business meetings all over the country, had crashed in fog over the Cumbrian mountains, killing both Alex and his assistant instantly. But just because Alex had died it didn't alter the fact that Wolf had hated the cut-and-thrust of Alex's business world as he built up the family empire, that it had made

Wolf shudder just to think of being involved in that world himself. And now, it appeared, he wasn't just involved in it; he had become more of a cold-hearted bastard than Alex had ever been!

'You can't marry Rebecca because it makes good business sense, Wolf——'

'Who says I can't? You?' he challenged scornfully. 'You bailed out of my life at the first sign that things might be tough for a while, so don't——'

'That isn't true!' Cyn gasped incredulously. 'I didn't have any choice. You——'

'Yes?' he grated viciously. 'I what? Wouldn't be able to give you the attention you wanted after Alex died so suddenly?' he dismissed contemptuously. 'I thought you'd understand how it had to be.' He shook his head disgustedly. 'But you didn't leave me with that erroneous belief for long, did you! Oh, no, you decided then was the perfect time to tell me you were seeing Collins again.' His eyes glittered now with remembered anger at the disclosure. 'If you ever *stopped* seeing him,' he added harshly.

'And just what do you mean by that?' she demanded, heated colour darkening her cheeks.

Wolf made a dismissive movement with his hands. 'You were involved with Collins before I met you. We were—close, ourselves, only a few weeks; it's only natural to assume that—— '

'I was continuing to see Roger at the same time I was telling you I loved you!' she finished accusingly, her eyes gleaming deeply violet. 'Credit me with a few more morals than you had yourself, Wolf,' she scorned with distaste.

His eyes narrowed to amber slits. 'Meaning?'

'Meaning——' Cyn broke off with a heavy sigh. She wasn't in the least disconcerted by the obvious danger of his chilling anger—at least, not much!—it was just that she couldn't see the point, now of all times, of raking up the painful events of the past. 'It doesn't matter.' She shook her head dismissively.

'Obviously it does.' His eyes were still narrowed. 'Otherwise you wouldn't have made the remark at all.' His hands moved to grasp the tops of her arms as he held her securely in front of him.

Not that he needed to have bothered to have held her so tightly; her legs had gone too weak, at the first touch of his hands, to support her moving away!

'Tell me what you meant, Cyn,' he said abruptly. 'I'm not leaving here until you do.'

She gazed up at him with pained eyes. God, she had once loved this man so much, had been willing to do anything for him—except the one thing he had demanded of her, she remembered heavily. Roger had tried to warn her, when she first went out with Wolf, had told her that people of Wolf Thornton's class lived by a different set of rules from them. Only she had been too much in love, even then, to want to listen to those warnings. It had been a reluctance she had paid for a long time after Wolf was completely out of her life!

He was so close to her now, the warmth of his breath gently stirring the wispy blond fringe of hair on her forehead, the smell of his aftershave, a light woodsy smell, along with that masculine smell that was pure Wolf, filling her senses, making further thought impossible for the moment.

Or resistance, as she felt herself being slowly drawn towards the hard strength of his chest, the long length of his legs already pressed against hers.

'Cyn...!' he groaned low in his throat, the sound almost primeval, his arms moving about her now like steel bands as he drew her into the seductive warmth of his body.

It was as if the years since Wolf last held her like this had never been, her lips parting instinctively for the depth of his kiss, the onslaught fierce and demanding, his lips grinding down on hers, his hands roving restlessly down the length of her spine before coming to rest possessively against her hips, holding her against the taut arousal of his own body.

Wolf wanted her! As much as he ever had, Cyn realised dazedly. But even as she knew the truth of that she felt her own quivering response to the now languid caress of his lips against hers, tasting her, the tip of his tongue brailling every centimetre of her lips before dipping fleetingly into the hot, moist cavern beneath. Again. And again. Those flickering caresses were driving her into a frenzy of need for something deeper, her legs felt weak as she clung to the broad strength of his shoulders, her fingers unknowingly digging into the hard flesh there.

She trembled against him as his lips left hers now to travel the length of her throat, moving moistly against the throbbing column there, and her breath caught in her throat, her head falling back weakly against her shoulders.

This couldn't be happening, was totally wrong, she knew in her more sane moments, and yet there was no way she could bring a halt to these caresses. Her whole being was crying out in need for the only man she had ever wanted in this way.

Wolf raised his head slowly, looking down at her, his eyes flowing liquid gold now, a nerve pulsing against the full sensuality of his mouth, the warmth of his hands burning through the silky material of Cyn's blouse as he still held her against him.

Her tongue flickered out to moisten lips that had gone suddenly dry at the passionate intensity of that amber gaze, her breath leaving her in a shuddering sigh as she saw the way Wolf's eyes darkened at her unknowingly provocative movement. 'Wolf, I——' She broke off with a disbelieving groan as the telephone on her desk began to ring intrusively.

She didn't want to answer the call; she wanted to find out what emotion, if any, had motivated Wolf into kissing her in the way that he had. The passionate intensity of his kisses had been unmistakable, as had been her own instinctive response. But even as she looked up at him, to form her question, he was pushing her away from him, a hard savagery to the lips that had moved against her so sensually only seconds earlier.

He moved away from her with abrupt movements. 'Answer the damn thing!' he instructed harshly, glaring. 'After all,' his mouth twisted, 'it might be some poor bride wanting to run away from her wedding, and everything connected with it—including the bridegroom!'

Cyn's cheeks flushed as she remembered her conversation with Rebecca Harcourt such a short time ago. If ever a bride looked poised to run, it had been her!

And if the Wolf Cyn had seen today—those kisses apart!—was the one Rebecca knew, then Cyn didn't blame her for feeling that way!

She reached automatically for the telephone receiver, all the time her puzzled gaze resting on Wolf as he stood so remote across the room, staring out of the window down on to the street below now. The office was situated above a bakery in the small shopping precinct. There were some days when the smell of baking permeating from the shop below could drive Cyn wild with hunger, but, despite the fact that it was almost two-thirty and she hadn't even had lunch yet, today was not one of those days! And she doubted that Wolf was actually seeing any of the shopping scene below him either. Unless he had grown more heartless than she had imagined— because she still felt like a quivering wreck after the kisses they had shared!

'Hello, Cyn,' greeted a warm, masculine voice after she had put the receiver up to her ear and given the name of the agency. 'You shot off earlier before I had a chance to make definite plans to meet you for that dinner you promised me,' he added reprovingly.

Gerald Harcourt! Cyn shot a self-conscious glance across the room at Wolf. Of all the people who could have called her now...!

As if becoming aware of her tension, Wolf slowly turned to look at her, that amber gaze deeply probing on her suddenly pale face. 'What is it?' He frowned suspiciously.

Cyn swallowed hard. This was awful, just awful! She didn't know what to do.

'Cyn?' Gerald prompted with a puzzled voice as he received no response to his teasingly made statement. 'Have I called at a bad time?' he guessed astutely.

A bad time! It couldn't have been any worse. She swallowed hard. 'Not really,' she lied. 'And dinner would be lovely.' She deliberately didn't look at Wolf as she accepted the invitation; if she hadn't accepted it, she would have just prolonged the conversation, and with Wolf in the room, his expression now thunderous, that was the last thing she wanted to do. 'Could you pick me up at eight o'clock?' she continued to speak briskly to Gerald. 'There's a rather good Italian restaurant quite near here we could go to. Unless you would rather not have pasta?' Who cared whether or not he cared for pasta? She just wanted to get this conversation over with as quickly as possible. Because if she didn't, she had a feeling Wolf was going to explode!

'Pasta sounds marvellous,' Gerald agreed quickly, obviously pleased at his speedy success when he had surely been envisaging having to persuade her into accepting his invitation.

Cyn quickly gave him her address, all the time keeping a wary eye on Wolf, and ringing off as soon as she was able without appearing rude to Gerald.

Wolf hadn't moved from his position in front of the window, and yet he seemed to have grown, become even more intimidating—if that were possible! Cyn stood beside her desk, her hands clasped self-consciously together in front of her, watching him warily. Both of them were silent, Cyn because she simply didn't know what to say, Wolf, she was sure, because he had too much to say!

'Gerald?' he finally accused knowingly.

'Yes,' she replied unnecessarily; the flush that had instantly darkened her cheeks had been confirmation enough.

Wolf's mouth tightened ominously. 'And you're having dinner with him tonight.'

Her chin rose in an instinctively defensive movement. 'Yes,' she abruptly acknowledged the statement.

He shook his head, his mouth turned back scornfully. 'You asked me a short time ago what happened to me,' he bit out derisively. 'I can tell you in one word what happened to me, Cyn,' he rasped harshly. 'You happened to me! You with your silver hair, violet-blue eyes, and such an expression of innocence I was totally fooled

seven years ago. But not again, Cyn.' He marched purposefully over to the door and wrenched it open. 'Never
again!' He slammed the door so forcefully after his exit
that the whole room seemed to vibrate in reaction.

Cyn finally gave in to the weakness in her legs and
sat down heavily in her chair behind the desk.

'Never again', Wolf had said. And yet his kisses such
a short time ago, in this very room, made a lie of that
claim. In fact, if Wolf could kiss *her* with such passion
then he had no right marrying Rebecca Harcourt at all!

CHAPTER THREE

IN THE ordinary course of events, she and Wolf would never have met at all. In fact, it might have been better for everyone concerned if they never had!

Cyn had been working as one of the evening receptionists at Thornton's, the exclusive hotel the family owned in the centre of London—the same hotel Rebecca and Wolf were due to hold their wedding reception at in August, which was why they knew there would be no problem with *that* particular booking!

There had been a lot of day as well as night-time staff on duty that particular evening; Alex Thornton and his wife were hosting a sixtieth birthday party for his mother, Claudia, in the main function-room. Despite the fact that this was posted up on the notice-board as the guests entered the hotel, Cyn had spent the majority of the beginning of the evening directing people to the appropriate room. Not that she had seen any of the family themselves; they had been escorted into the party by the manager himself. By ten-fifteen, Cyn had been sure all the guests had to be present by now, and settled down at her computer console to complete some of the paperwork that seemed to go along with the job and which she hadn't had time to deal with earlier, while several of the other girls on duty took a well-earned break; they had all been working extremely hard today to make sure everything ran smoothly for the Thornton party. Cyn had been quite happy to wait for her own break. Besides, she knew she wasn't going to be too

popular if the couple in Room 217 weren't even of-
ficially registered, let alone their preference for morning
newspapers logged in!

'What did that computer ever do to you?' queried a
deeply amused voice.

Cyn looked up from her frowning concentration on
the VDU, her eyes widening as she took in the appearance of the man leaning so casually over the top of
the desk as he watched her struggling to squash a lengthy
home address of one of the guests into the totally in-
adequate space given for this very purpose by the supposedly foolproof computer program; obviously they
hadn't considered people coming from Russia when they
devised the program. But one look at this man and she
didn't care whether the address was legible enough, after
her pruning, for the guest to be billed for any extras
discovered after his departure or not. This man was
gorgeous!

Tall—he had to be, to be able to lean this far over the
top of the reception-desk!—with over-long blond hair
that persisted in falling forward over his high intelligent
forehead, eyes the colour of warm amber looking at Cyn
with deepening amusement as she continued to stare at
him, his features striking rather than what could strictly
be called handsome, everything slightly larger than life,
his cheekbones high, his nose slightly bent, as if it might
have been broken at some time, his mouth—— Oh, God,
that mouth...!

Cyn stood up slowly, crossing to stand on the other
side of the desk from him. 'Machines and I don't get
on,' she dismissed with a rueful shrug. 'Can I help you?'
she offered politely, although from the look of his black
evening suit and snowy white shirt, his black bow-tie
spoiling the immaculate effect slightly, being not quite

straight, as if he had tied it in a hurry, he was yet another guest for the Thornton party. She couldn't help wondering if one of the other girls would know who this particular guest was. There was a list, of course, for security reasons, but that seemed to have been put to one side earlier as they were swamped with queries about the party. Cyn gave it a sideways glance as it lay on the desk by her hand, but there were so many names not crossed off that it would be impossible to know who this man was. Unless she asked him. And she couldn't do that— much as she longed to!

'I hope so,' he grimaced. 'I'm afraid I'm a little late, you see, and——'

'The Thornton party,' she nodded understandingly. 'Well, I shouldn't worry too much about being late, if I were you; there are so many people crushed into that room that I doubt if anyone has noticed your absence!' Although if *she* had asked this man to a party, even if there were three hundred other guests invited, she would still have noticed his absence.

His grimace deepened. 'I wouldn't be too sure of that if I were you!' He shook his head.

Ah, she thought, there was obviously a woman involved, a woman who, like her, would be well aware of his absence. A woman he obviously didn't want to hurt, otherwise he wouldn't have been here at all, Cyn would hazard a guess. For some reason that knowledge made her feel slightly depressed.

'I'd forgotten it was tonight at all, you see,' the man frowned, completely unaware of Cyn's disappointed thoughts. 'Until about half an hour ago. I must have made the quickest change in history, and—— What is it?' He frowned as he saw she was slowly nodding at his words.

Her cheeks felt slightly warm as she blushed slightly. 'I was—well, I was just thinking that that accounts for it,' she admitted awkwardly.

Dark blond brows rose. 'Accounts for what?' he said slowly.

It was hardly her place to tell one of the hotel guests he was less than immaculately dressed! 'I—— Well—— You see——'

He frowned down at his own appearance as he realised this was what seemed to be causing her embarrassment. 'Hell, I haven't put odd socks on again, have I?—no, that can't be it,' he ruefully answered his own suggestion. 'You can't see as far down as my feet. All right,' he sighed, 'what is it? Blood on my shirt collar? Shaving foam in my ears? Blood on my shirt collar *and* shaving foam in my ears?' he groaned desperately.

Cyn was laughing by this time; she couldn't help it. Because from his self-derisive attitude to the suggestion that he might have done any one—or all three!—of those things, she had a feeling that he had been guilty of all three of them on at least one occasion! 'None of those things,' she assured him, still smiling. 'Although your bow-tie is less than perfect,' she told him with a rueful grimace.

He put up a self-conscious hand to the offending item, a long, sensitive-looking hand, the fingers long and tapered. 'I never was any good with the damned things,' he muttered, looking up. 'I don't suppose you...?'

Cyn frowned her puzzlement. 'I what?'

'You can't be any worse at tying bow-ties than I am,' he decided firmly, leaning forward over the desk once again. 'Have a go,' he suggested, thrusting his chin forward to allow her better access to the tie at his throat.

She stared at him in dismay for several seconds. She couldn't just go around rearranging guests' dress! There was sure to be a rule about it somewhere in the contract she had signed to work here at all, and as she had only been here a matter of weeks——

'Well?' He muttered with his jaw clenched, obviously tiring of the unnatural pose. 'I could get a stiff neck if I have to hold my chin up much longer, and end up walking about like this all evening. Then I'll really be popular!'

With the woman at the Thorntons' party who was waiting for his arrival. But what was she worrying about? Cyn derided herself; she was never likely to see this man again, so what difference did it make to her who was waiting for him in that function-room!

'OK,' she sighed heavily, leaning forward to untie the bow so that she could start from scratch. From the look of the crushed material the rather sad-looking bow she had just undone had been far from his own first attempt this evening!

His proximity, necessarily so if she were to arrange the bow-tie at all, was more than a little unnerving! So much so that she made a complete mess of the bow herself the first time she tried. But the man was so close to her she could see the pores of his skin, the black flecks in those strange amber-coloured eyes, feel the warmth of his breath against her cheeks. How could she possibly be expected to concentrate?

'Not so easy, is it?' he said with satisfaction as she started again, luckily seeming to have no idea it was he himself who was making this so difficult for her.

'Mmm,' Cyn acknowledged as she frowned her attention on the bow-tie, her tongue sticking out between her teeth preventing her from making further conver-

sation as she tried her best to concentrate on tying the
bow rather than on the sensual magnetism of the man
she was tying it on.

He gave a sudden throaty chuckle. 'Anyone finding
us like this could be forgiven for completely misinter-
preting the situation—— I was only joking!' he protested as she moved sharply away, thrusting her hands
behind her back as if they had been stung. 'You can't
leave me half dressed like this!' he groaned as he put a
hand up and found the bow was still incomplete.

He was hardly 'half dressed', Cyn protested silently—
although the suggestion did bring some rather vivid im-
aginings to mind, predominantly a situation where he
actually *could* be 'half dressed'!

'Come here,' she instructed impatiently, pulling him
forward by the bow, her fingers moving deftly now, irritated with herself for indulging in such daydreams; this
man might be slightly disorganised, but he was still
someone important enough to be a guest at the Thornton
party, and, as such, completely out of her league.
'There!' she patted the newly tied bow-tie with satisfaction. 'You——'

'Wolf, what on earth are you doing?' demanded an
incredulous voice.

Cyn reacted with dismay to the sound of that intrusive
voice, sure she was going to be in trouble now over the
incident with the man she had now learnt was called
Wolf—Wolf...! What sort of a name was that, for
goodness' sake? He didn't look in the least perturbed by
the interruption, giving her a rueful grimace before
turning to face the woman who had called out to him.

'Enquiring where the party is, of course, Barbara,' he
drawled easily. 'How's it all going?' He strolled across
the reception area to join her.

Cyn looked closely at the other woman. She was one of the guests Cyn must have missed arriving earlier, because she didn't remember seeing her before. Beautiful— of course she would have to be!—her features smooth and even, dominated by enormous green eyes surrounded by thick sooty lashes, her mouth a pout of red, with a golden tan to her skin that she hadn't acquired in this country, not in the last few months, anyway. And with a cascade of ebony hair that tumbled down on to her shoulders in a style that was arranged to look completely casual but actually wasn't—Cyn did not doubt for a moment that it had taken an accomplished hairdresser several hours to achieve the effect. And she was tall, at least five feet eight even without the high-heeled shoes she wore with the figure-hugging black dress that showed a long expanse of her silken legs below its above-knee length.

Everything that Cyn herself wasn't, in fact, with her own almost waist-length hair secured in a single braid down her spine, and her pale elfin features that could never be called beautiful. And it had always been the bane of her life that she was only five feet tall in her stockinged feet; she had always longed to be tall and elegantly graceful. Like the woman Wolf was now kissing warmly on the cheek as he reached her side.

'Alex is getting more and more polite as the evening goes on,' the woman called Barbara tightly answered Wolf's light query, their conversation more than audible to Cyn as she stood at the reception-desk a short distance away, although she looked down awkwardly at some papers on top of the desk as flashing green eyes shot her a furious glare. 'A sure sign that he's absolutely furious!' the woman added with a frown.

Wolf sighed. 'When is he anything else these days?' He shook his head. 'He's going to give himself a heart attack if he carries on like this, Barbara. You know he——'

'He's furious with *you*, Wolf,' Barbara cut in impatiently. 'You know you should have been here with the rest of the family to greet our guests as they arrived!'

Alex? The rest of the family? *Our* guests? It suddenly dawned on Cyn, as she stood riveted to the spot, her stomach doing somersaults, that Wolf had to be a member of the Thornton family too, that Alex had to be Alex *Thornton*, the head of Thornton Industries; in effect, her own employer!

Oh, my God, she thought, and she had told Wolf no one would even notice he was missing from the party in the crush! And she had faulted his appearance before attempting to rearrange his bow-tie for him! Just who was he?

Dark blond brows rose mockingly over those amber eyes. 'As I received a formal invitation I thought I was included in the guest list, not the family,' he drawled derisively.

Barbara gave him a reproving frown, spoiling the beauty of her face as the frown gave her an almost primly disapproving look. 'You know you were sent the invitation so that it served as a reminder for you to come at all. Obviously we wasted our time even trying to do that!' She shook her head disgustedly. 'Oh, well, better late than never, I suppose.' She put her arm through the crook of his as she turned him purposefully in the direction of the room where the party was being held. 'Maybe when he sees you're here after all, Alex will start to calm down.'

'I wouldn't count on it,' Wolf murmured unconcernedly. 'Seeing me has never been known to have that effect on my too-serious brother before!'

Brother . . . ! It was worse than she had even imagined, Cyn realised. Wolf wasn't some obscure member of the Thornton family—which had been her fervent hope once she had realised he was related to them at all!—but was, in fact, the other son of the family, the one who had upset them all by becoming a musician or an artist, or something they considered equally unsuitable for a Thornton heir. Because that was certainly who he was— Wolf Thornton, joint heir with Alex Thornton to Thornton Industries, half-owner of this very hotel, in fact!

'No,' the woman called Barbara acknowledged with a rueful twist of those pouting red lips. 'But it will give your mother pleasure to have you here, and that's sure to help the situation.'

Wolf didn't look at all convinced by this method of thinking, and in fact Barbara didn't seem over-confident about it either. Having seen Alex Thornton several times, Cyn couldn't help but think they were right to be apprehensive; the two brothers not only looked nothing alike—Alex being much darker in colouring, with pale blue eyes that almost looked grey, and not possessing the impressive height of his brother—but the two men were nothing alike in temperament either, from the little she had seen of them. Alex Thornton was austere and unapproachable, while Wolf Thornton was possessed of a roguish charm that had instantly captivated Cyn.

In fact, she looked after him a little longingly as the woman Barbara led him away towards the function-room, where he would no doubt be swallowed up completely by the family and friends he had there, forgetting completely the young receptionist who had been so forward with him. Actually, she had better hope that he did exactly that where she was concerned; she didn't want to be sacked from this job just yet, and her manner towards him had hardly been professional!

Watching him now, so tall and impressive as he walked down the carpeted corridor at Barbara's side, she couldn't help but berate herself for not realising earlier that he had a presence, a self-confidence, that was an essential part of his make-up, had been inborn, in fact. But how could she have guessed he was Wolf Thornton? No one had ever mentioned what the other Thornton brother's first name was. And she certainly wouldn't have forgotten a name like Wolf if she had heard it before!

Suddenly he came to a halt, murmured something to the woman at his side, before turning and walking purposefully back towards the desk where Cyn still stood. She watched his progress towards her with increasingly widening eyes; oh, lord, what was he going to say to her now?

'Will you have dinner with me tomorrow evening— Lucynda Smith?' he added lightly after glancing at the name-badge on the lapel of the jacket the hotel had supplied as part of her uniform.

She swallowed hard, glancing past him towards the woman still standing in the corridor as she watched the two of them with narrowed green eyes, then hastily looked away again as she saw the venom in that glittering gaze, looking up at Wolf Thornton as if he had to have gone slightly mad—or she had; he hadn't really just invited her out to dinner tomorrow night—had he...?

'Cyn,' she answered automatically, dazedly.

He grinned, showing even white teeth against his tanned skin—a tan he had acquired at the same time as the lovely Barbara had? Cyn couldn't help wondering. Just who was the other woman? And what role did she have in Wolf's life if he could walk away from her to invite Cyn out for the evening?

'I didn't have sin in mind on our first date.' His eyes gleamed down at her with mocking humour. 'Only dinner.' He shrugged those broad shoulders. 'But if you insist I'm sure I could——'

'I meant my friends—people, call me Cyn. It's short for Lucynda,' she explained irritably as he still looked amused—at her expense! But who could really blame him? She was acting like a besotted teenager, not a responsible twenty-year-old.

'Ah,' his mouth twisted teasingly. 'Well, *Cyn*,' he drawled her name with deliberate intimacy, 'will you have dinner with me tomorrow evening? Nothing so grand as this place, I'm afraid.' He grimaced at their surroundings. 'I can only suffer this particular brand of opulence every couple of months or so!'

Cyn wouldn't have felt comfortable dining anywhere like this hotel herself. But she couldn't have dinner anywhere with this man: he was her employer, for goodness' sake, albeit in a non-participating capacity; she had heard that the second son of the Thornton family kept well away from the business side of things.

She shook her head. 'I can't, I'm afraid.'

'Working,' he nodded understandingly. 'I could ask my brother to arrange for you to have the evening off,' he said lightly, 'but——'

'Oh, no!' Cyn gasped her dismay at the very suggestion. The last thing she wanted was for the head of the Thornton family to hear of her encounter with his brother!

'—I won't,' Wolf finished mockingly. 'I think the best thing to do is work out which evening you *do* have free, and arrange things from there, don't you?'

Cyn looked up at him searchingly. He didn't seem to be taunting her, and yet—— Why on earth was he inviting out a little nonentity like her?

'Do you like Chinese food?' he added temptingly. 'It's my passion at the moment. If you would rather——'

'I love Chinese food,' Cyn told him hastily, very conscious of the growing impatience of the beautiful Barbara as she now stood in the corridor, tapping her elegantly-shod foot against the marble floor. 'And as it happens I do have tomorrow evening off. But——'

'Great! I'll meet you outside here at seven-thirty tomorrow evening,' he said economically, having glanced round to see that a man had now joined the lovely Barbara—a man Cyn recognised only too well as Alex Thornton himself! 'I hate to eat late,' Wolf told Cyn before striding off to join the other couple, not looking at her again as the three of them went off in the direction of the music.

Cyn stared after him dazedly. She had just been bull-dozed, railroaded, bullied—in the nicest possible way!—into meeting Wolf Thornton for dinner tomorrow evening!

She should never have kept that date with him, should have realised getting to know him any better than she already had would only lead to heartache. Oh, heartache didn't even begin to describe the pain she had suffered for daring to fall in love with Wolf Thornton!

Having dinner with Gerald Harcourt that evening was much less traumatic. Gerald was easy company, flirtatious without being pushy—perhaps because he didn't usually have to be, Cyn thought a little indulgently; Gerald's good looks and charm would normally make it all too easy for him to make conquests. Just not Cyn. Oh, she liked him well enough, and if he hadn't been going to be Wolf's father-in-law, she might even have kept on seeing him on a casual basis. But as he *was* going to be Wolf's father-in-law...!

'I'm not giving up on you,' he told her warmly when she refused his second invitation for dinner. 'I happen to think you could be the woman who changes my opinion about marriage.'

Cyn looked up at him reprovingly as they stood inside the tiny sitting-room of the small two-bedroomed cottage she had taken a lease on a couple of years ago in the countryside several miles outside Feltham itself, Gerald having driven her home after their meal. 'Do many women fall for that line?' she drawled derisively.

He grinned unabashedly. 'Quite a few, actually,' he acknowledged derisively.

She chuckled wryly. 'Well, not me, Mr Harcourt,' she told him firmly. 'If anything I'm probably less kindly disposed towards marriage than you are,' she added.

'You see?' Gerald still smiled, completely unperturbed. 'We're perfect for each other!'

Cyn chuckled softly, warmly returning his humour. 'Forget it, Gerald,' she drawled. 'Maybe we can have dinner again another time, but for the moment I prefer to concentrate on your daughter's wedding.'

He gave a grimace. 'Reminding me I have a daughter old enough to be married puts me firmly in my place, doesn't it?' he acknowledged ruefully.

She shook her head. 'I didn't mean it to sound that way. I—— Your daughter's very young to be getting married,' she added as casually as she was able—when it was Wolf that Rebecca intended marrying.

Gerald frowned. 'She's over twenty. Admittedly Wolf is a lot older than her, thirty-five, but I'm sure they'll be good for each other.' He shook his head at her implied suggestion that perhaps they wouldn't.

'The bridegroom did seem a little—remote,' she said awkwardly. The Wolf she had met today bore little or no resemblance to that teasing man she had met seven years ago; he didn't look as if he knew *how* to tease!

'Oh, Wolf's all right,' Gerald dismissed comfortably. 'He and Rebecca are good friends.'

'Friends?' Cyn frowned at his choice of words. 'Isn't that a strange thing to say about a couple who intend marrying in four months' time?'

'Not in the least strange,' Gerald disagreed. 'I only wish Rebecca's mother and I had been friends before we married, maybe then we wouldn't have ended up hating each other's guts once the initial passion wore a little thin. The same goes for you, I'd hazard a guess.' He looked at her shrewdly.

Her eyes widened. 'What do you mean?' she asked warily. What *did* he mean? She was sure, not by word or deed, that she and Wolf hadn't given away the fact earlier today that they had known each other years ago.

Gerald shrugged. 'Whoever the man was in your past, who gave you the same distrust of marriage that I have, I'll bet the two of you weren't friends.'

It was a bet he would lose. She and Wolf had been great friends, had found a rapport existed between the two of them from the first—much to Cyn's surprise; she had been sure the two of them could have nothing in common. But there was no way she could tell Gerald that Wolf had been that man!

She smiled dismissively. 'I'm sure we all have disastrous love-affairs in our past that have coloured our judgement in later life,' she shrugged. 'We get over them.' She held her chin defensively high, knowing she had never got over loving Wolf.

'Some of us do,' Gerald nodded thoughtfully, watching her closely. 'I'll take a rain-check on the dinner invitation, then,' he finally accepted lightly, moving to grasp her gently by the upper arms. 'But I really meant it when I said I'm not giving up on you.' He kissed her lightly on the lips.

Cyn stood in the doorway of the brightly lit cottage waving goodbye to Gerald as he drove away, wondering exactly what he would make of the fact that seven years ago she had been the one about to marry Wolf!

Given time—once she finally got away from the hotel that evening, without seeing Wolf Thornton again, unfortunately—Cyn had decided that he couldn't really have been serious about the dinner invitation. But if she had thought he hadn't been serious, what on earth had possessed her to be waiting outside the Thornton's Hotel at seven-thirty the following evening?

She had felt very conspicuous standing outside on the pavement, several people entering the hotel eyeing her curiously as she did her best to look casually unconcerned by the obvious fact that she was waiting for someone. Someone who, by seven-forty, still hadn't arrived!

He *hadn't* been serious, she realised with a sinking heart, wondering how she could slip away without drawing any more attention to herself. The doorman, a

man she had come to know over the last few weeks, had
been watching surreptitiously to see just who her date
was for the evening. How awful that the 'date' hadn't
turned up!

'Thank God I caught you!' gasped a breathless voice
behind her. 'I thought I was going to be too late.'

Cyn had been in the act of quietly slipping away from
the front entrance of the hotel, but she turned sharply
at the first sound of Wolf Thornton's voice.

If she hadn't been sure what to wear for their date,
formal or casual, then Wolf seemed to have been even
less sure. He was wearing no jacket at all, despite the
brisk breeze on this April evening, and his shirt had come
adrift from the faded denims he wore—and he seemed
to have the remains of a meal down the front of the pale
blue shirt! At least—she frowned at the vivid red and
green streaks—she *presumed* it was a meal?

His appearance was certainly much less formal than
it had been on Saturday evening, and his hair was hope-
lessly windswept, not with that deliberate casualness that
was so much in fashion nowadays, but actually blown
in complete disarray by the breeze.

A fact he seemed to become conscious of as she continued to look at him silently, putting up an impatient
hand to smooth the errant dark blond locks from his
brow. 'I really am sorry I'm late for our date, Cyn,' he
told her with a rueful grimace. 'But I—— Well, I got
caught up in work, and——'

'You work on a Sunday?' She couldn't help her
surprise.

He grinned at her reaction. 'I work every day, Cyn.'
He took a firm grasp of one of her arms. 'Let's go and
eat—we can talk over our meal,' he suggested cajolingly.

He thought she was going to refuse to have dinner with him at all because he was over ten minutes late! Cyn realised dazedly. She hadn't been very happy about having to stand in such a conspicuous place as she waited for him, she admitted—and, now that he had arrived, Ron, the doorman, was completely agog at just who had turned up to meet her, obviously recognising Wolf from last night!—but she was far too curious about this enigmatic man to change her mind about having dinner with him just because of that. And from Ron's almost stunned expression, the sooner they moved away from the hotel the better!

'I thought you might have already eaten...?' She frowned up at Wolf as she moved with him to the taxi he had signalled to come over to them.

Wolf gave the driver an address before joining Cyn in the back of the taxi, looking puzzled as he turned to look at her. 'What on earth gave you that——? This isn't food,' he dismissed with a laugh as he saw the direction her gaze had taken, putting up a self-conscious hand to the marks on his shirt. 'I should have changed before coming to meet you,' he acknowledged with a grimace. 'But I was so caught up in what I was doing, it was almost seven-thirty before I even remembered our date—I didn't put that very well, did I?' He winced as he saw her mockingly raised brows.

She laughed softly, starting to relax now that they were away from the hotel; it was the worst possible place they could have agreed to meet, although she acknowledged that, at the time, they hadn't had much time to think of another location. 'It wasn't the most flattering thing you could have said,' she shook her head with a rueful smile.

Wolf's hands moved to clasp one of hers. 'Once you've known me for a while, you'll realise that flattery is one thing I never give,' he told her with intensity. 'In fact, I've been accused of the opposite on more than one occasion.' He seemed to deliberately lighten the conversation. 'I hope you don't mind, but I've asked the driver to take us to my flat; I really should change before taking you out to dinner!'

Cyn didn't care where they went; her body was doing strange things just at the touch of his hand on hers, and she could see that awareness reflecting in the warm amber of Wolf's eyes as they made the journey to his flat.

The flat, as she should have guessed, was in Mayfair, and Wolf took her up in the almost silent lift to the penthouse apartment at the top of the building. But the furniture, she saw as they stepped straight into the luxurious lounge, ebony and chrome, the suite of dark brown leather, somehow didn't look like Wolf at all. Which was a ridiculous thing for her to think. What did she know of this man's tastes in——?

'Barbara's idea of what my apartment should be furnished like,' Wolf told her with a dismissive grimace as he seemed to guess her thoughts.

Barbara again. Cyn couldn't help wondering exactly where the other woman fitted into his life—because she obviously did fit into it somewhere. Somehow that knowledge made her feel strangely depressed.

Wolf seemed unaware of her feelings this time. 'Give me a few minutes to change and I'll be with you,' he promised lightly. 'Help yourself to a drink,' he waved vaguely in the direction of the drinks cabinet across the room. 'And feel free to peruse the bookshelves,' he added before hurrying from the room, already unbuttoning his shirt as he went.

Cyn took a few minutes to catch her breath before taking him up on either of those offers; being in the company of Wolf Thornton was a little like being ushered along by an express train!

But when she did finally look at the extensive bookshelves along one wall of the room—she wasn't interested in the drink, she rarely drank alcohol anyway, and never on an empty stomach—she found Wolf's taste in books as lively as his mind, the subject matter ranging from poetry, autobiographies, both historic and fairly recent, to art and history. His taste in fiction was almost as varied; thrillers, fantasy, mysteries, even the occasional novel which she would have classed as romance. Admittedly the latter were usually the classics, but nevertheless Cyn still thought it would be difficult to tell the nature of the man from his taste in books. And even in the short time she had known him, it had become very important to her that she should come to know more about him, *much* more about him.

But Wolf's 'few minutes' stretched into much longer than that, until a glance at her wristwatch told her he had been gone at least half an hour. Surely it didn't take him this long to change his clothes? Even if, at the last minute, he had decided to shower and shave before he put on fresh clothes, it surely wouldn't have taken him as long as this?

'Wolf?' she called out tentatively. 'Wolf!' she said more firmly when she received no answer to her first call. Still no answer. What on earth was the man doing?

She didn't exactly feel comfortable with the idea of going into his bedroom, but if he wasn't going to answer her when she called . . . ! Besides, for all she knew, he might have fallen or something, and be unable to answer her. It wasn't very likely, she admitted, but something had to be delaying him.

The 'something' turned out to be a total surprise. Cyn had had no idea...!

Wolf's bedroom—another room she would say hadn't been decorated or furnished by him, the cool blues and heavy ornate furniture not suiting him at all—was empty of the man himself, as was the adjoining bathroom. But the other adjoining door she discovered across the room proved more fruitful.

She entered the room slowly, tentatively, her eyes widening as she found herself in a studio, an artist's studio. Paintings finished and half finished, leant against every bit of wall-space. The roof of the room was mainly glass, to allow the maximum of light, Cyn would guess, light needed to paint the vivid scenes that assaulted all the senses, not just the optical ones, as she gazed around the room at them in increasing wonder. The paintings were good, very good, even to her untutored eye. And *Wolf* had painted them...

The man himself sat with his back towards her, obviously totally engrossed in the half-completed canvas in front of him, the woman in the picture lying like a siren across the grey rocks as the even greyer sea thundered around her, trying to tear her into its silky depths. Silver-blond hair swirled in the savage wind, the woman's pale blue dress clung wetly to the sensual curves outlined beneath. Cyn's gaze returned to the woman's face, to the serene expression, the elfin face dominated by deeply violet-coloured eyes... There was something familiar about the woman, something—— My God, she thought, it was *her*!

She must have gasped out loud at the realisation, because Wolf turned sharply, his gaze glazed and unseeing for a few brief seconds, and then he seemed to focus on her, shaking his head self-disgustedly. 'My God, I've done it again, haven't I?' He stood up abruptly, wiping paint from his hands on to a cloth that looked as if it wasn't the first time he had done so today, what had once been a white cloth now covered in—— It was *paint* Wolf had on his shirt too, Cyn suddenly realised; he must have been working on this painting before he came to meet her. *This* was the reason he had forgotten their date.

And the woman in the painting was her, she was sure of it...

Wolf saw the puzzlement in her face, as he crossed the room to stand in front of her. 'Yes, it's you,' he confirmed softly. 'It's the main reason I was late meeting you this evening.'

Cyn still stared at the half-finished painting. 'You were busy working on it,' she nodded dazedly.

'I have been since I got home last night.' He was also looking at the painting. 'But it wasn't just that.' He moved to gently clasp her shoulders, his expression intense as he looked down at her. 'While I was working on the painting time seemed to stand still, go nowhere, and I——' He shook his head. 'When I told you earlier I'd forgotten our date, I didn't mean I'd really forgotten it, only that the time had slipped away from me. God, I've been longing to see you again since I left you last night. Do you believe in destiny, Cyn?' he prompted forcefully, shaking her slightly when she didn't immediately answer him. 'I'm not sure that I did. Until last night. Painting is my life, Cyn, I've wanted to do nothing else—have *done* nothing else—since I can remember.' He was talking quickly, desperate in his need to make her understand. 'And I've been satisfied, even pleased at times—no mean feat, believe me; I'm my own hardest critic!—with some of the work I've done in the past. But last night, when I could finally get away from the party, I was inspired. I knew I had to put you on canvas, knew exactly *how* I had to put you on canvas too.' He gazed across the room at the painting. 'It's good, Cyn.' His face glowed with the satisfaction of knowing he spoke the truth.

And he did, Cyn couldn't argue with that. The painting was beautiful, hauntingly so. But what did it mean? Why had Wolf painted her in that way?

'I'm getting these paintings ready for my first exhibition due to take place in the summer,' he told her now. 'I wanted—needed—something special as the main subject of that exhibition.' He looked back at the painting. 'This painting is going to be it.'

Cyn dragged her own gaze away from the hauntingly hypnotic painting, looking up at Wolf as he once again became engrossed in the half-completed canvas; it was obvious, even now, that it was going to be a painting worthy of the title 'something special', and that had nothing to do with the fact that Wolf had painted her to look so beautiful. There was a magic quality about all Wolf's work, but this one . . . ! Cyn didn't doubt that the exhibition was going to be a success for him, that the name Thornton was going to be associated with much more than the business world by the end of the year, that Wolf Thornton, the artist, was going to become known worldwide.

'I'm glad meeting me was able to give you that,' she told him shyly.

He turned to look at her, shaking off the hypnotic quality of the painting, a warm smile lighting his perfectly hewn features as he once again clasped her arms. 'Oh, it gave me much more than the painting, Cyn,' he assured her firmly. 'It gave me the woman I'm going to marry!'

She felt as if all the breath had been knocked from her lungs. Her mouth went dry, every muscle in her body was tense with disbelief. He couldn't really have said . . .

'Destiny, Cyn,' he reminded her teasingly, laughing down affectionately at her pole-axed expression. 'I wasn't just talking about the inspiration for the painting,' he rebuked gently. 'It was meeting the woman I wanted to make my wife that gave me that inspiration!'

'Me?' she squeaked. She couldn't believe this man— his background as a Thornton apart, if it ever could be!—a man who, if he really believed in destiny, must know he was destined to be one of the greatest artists of the day, actually wanted to marry *her*.

He didn't know anything about her, or her early years in an orphanage, even more years than that in different foster-homes, the time after that when she had struggled to attain even enough secretarial qualifications to get suitable work. Her job as receptionist at Thornton's Hotel was her most prestigious yet. And now the man who half owned that hotel was telling her he had taken one look at her and decided he wanted to marry her. It was unbelievable!

'You, Lucynda Smith,' he confirmed determinedly. 'And before my exhibition goes on I'm going to convince you that *you* want to marry *me* too!'

And he had convinced her, effortlessly; it had been impossible not to fall in love with him, to be there when he needed her. The two of them spent every moment they could together from that very first night, to make sure he didn't forget to eat altogether when he became engrossed in his painting—she had finally gone out that first evening and bought them a take-away Chinese meal!—to marvel in the passion of his lovemaking, their physical response to each other almost overwhelming in its intensity.

By the end of their first month together the painting of Cyn had been completed even to Wolf's own exacting demands—and Cyn had proudly worn his engagement ring on her finger.

She knew exactly what had happened to that sapphire and diamond engagement ring; she had given it back to him only weeks later.

But what had happened to the painting of her? And the other paintings he had had completed in his studio too? Because there had been no exhibition of Wolf's work during that summer, or any other as far as Cyn was aware. And she had looked out for Wolf Thornton paintings during the following years, had both dreaded, and longed, to see his work again. But there had been no Wolf Thornton paintings on display, ever.

What had happened to *Wolf*...?

CHAPTER FOUR

'WOLF can be—difficult,' Rebecca told her awkwardly.

Tell me about it, Cyn thought ruefully, remembering all too clearly that last conversation she had had with him. Not that she could tell this girl about that.

The two of them had met for lunch as arranged, and almost as soon as their food had been ordered Rebecca had launched into an explanation as to why she had thought it best to talk to Cyn in privacy concerning her wish not to hurry the wedding arrangements. Cyn had sat quietly and listened to it all during the soup course— the claim again that there was plenty of time yet until the wedding, that the invitations didn't need to go out for weeks yet, that Rebecca knew exactly what sort of wedding-gown she wanted, bridesmaid's dresses too, and they could all be made a bit nearer the time. Besides, Rebecca had added lightly, she wanted to lose a bit of weight before the wedding, which only meant the wedding-gown would have to be altered to fit her if it were made now.

Looking at her, at Rebecca's slenderness already bordering on delicacy, Cyn didn't think the other girl needed to lose any weight at all, just as she didn't think any of these excuses had anything to do with Rebecca's request for space and time over the wedding arrangements. Although she still hoped the young gardener wasn't the real reason for Rebecca's reluctance to get the wedding arrangements under way.

'Difficult?' she echoed the girl's description now, Rebecca having once again been defending the fact that she would rather Wolf knew nothing of this conversation.

A flush darkened Rebecca's cheeks, almost the same vivid red as her shoulder-length hair. 'He wouldn't understand my need for—well, less haste,' she explained awkwardly. 'He might think it was a reluctance to marry him at all that's prompted these—feelings.' She couldn't quite seem to meet Cyn's sympathetic gaze.

'And might he be right?' Cyn prompted gently.

'Certainly not!' Rebecca protested instantly—too instantly? 'I've told you my reasons for not wanting to be rushed.' She was becoming agitated now, absently crumbling the bread roll that had accompanied her soup, seeming unaware of the fact that she was totally demolishing it. 'Wolf is a wonderful man. Wonderful,' she repeated shakily. 'And he cares for me very much.'

'And you?' Cyn watched the younger girl with narrowed eyes; there was something very wrong here, no matter what Rebecca might try to claim to the contrary. 'Do you care for him very much in return?'

'Of course,' Rebecca told her defensively, her eyes deeply blue. 'Why else would I be marrying him?' she asked lightly.

Why else, indeed? Cyn's feelings of unease about the whole situation had increased as she talked to Rebecca, and she had not been reassured. She didn't doubt for a moment that Rebecca truly cared about Wolf, the affection was there in her voice when she talked of him, but did she care for him the way a bride should care about the man she was going to marry in four months' time? That was the question. And it was one Cyn wasn't really in a position to ask without totally offending someone who should, after all, have been just another client to her. The fact that Rebecca wasn't, and, in the circumstances, never could be, was something the girl was totally unaware of. And would remain unaware of!

She gave Rebecca a warm smile, trying her best to relax her as their soup bowls were removed and their main course was brought over to them; although if Rebecca ate as much of that as she had the soup and roll they might as well remove the plate now! Which posed another question; was Rebecca's appetite always this tiny, or was it the strain she was obviously under that was causing it?

'Maybe you should try talking to your fiancé about this,' Cyn broached again cautiously. 'He's sure to understand if you explain—— No?' she frowned as Rebecca shook her head at the suggestion before she had even finished.

'It isn't only Wolf,' Rebecca sighed. 'Daddy would be so disappointed if——' She chewed on her bottom lip, looking very unhappy. 'He and Wolf are great friends.'

That was exactly what Gerald had claimed about Rebecca and Wolf! But no matter what Gerald might think to the contrary, people who were friends, just friends, shouldn't really be contemplating marrying each other. Not when the girl involved obviously had more than a passing interest in her father's gardener... And the more Cyn talked to Rebecca the more convinced she became that *this* was the main reason for the other girl's reluctance to start her wedding arrangements. The mere idea of it seemed to make it too real to her...!

'Your father isn't the one marrying Wolf,' she pointed out drily.

Rebecca gave a wan smile in answer to Cyn's attempt at humour. 'No,' she acknowledged slowly. 'I had the distinct impression that my father's interest lay somewhere else entirely.' She gave Cyn a speculative glance.

Rebecca's own emotions might be in turmoil, but obviously that hadn't prevented her being well aware of what was going on in her father's life too! And how neatly she had turned the tables on Cyn. Maybe this girl *was* a fitting wife for Wolf, after all; she certainly knew how to stand up for herself when the situation presented itself.

Cyn's cheeks were the ones to feel hot now. 'Your father and I had dinner together last night, yes, but——'

'You didn't tell him we were meeting today, did you?' Rebecca put in quickly, instantly looking worried.

'No,' Cyn reassured her. 'Although I think perhaps you should,' she added softly.

'Why?' The other girl eyed her warily.

Cyn looked at her with gentle rebuke. 'I think you know why, Rebecca—— You don't mind if I call you Rebecca, do you?' she prompted lightly.

'Well, as you're dating my father it would be a little——'

'I'm not dating your father, Rebecca,' Cyn told her firmly, determined not to be put on the defensive, which she was sure Rebecca was trying to do in an effort to divert the attention away from the real issue, an issue they had been skirting around all during lunch—and that was that Rebecca, for all she obviously liked and respected Wolf, certainly didn't want to marry him! 'I've been out with him once, because I half promised that I would, but I'm not expecting to repeat it.'

Rebecca's eyes widened at her certainty, a rueful smile suddenly lighting her lovely features. 'That must have been a surprise for Daddy,' she chuckled softly.

Cyn returned the smile. 'I believe it was!'

'Poor Daddy!' Rebecca shook her head.

'Look, Rebecca,' Cyn sobered, leaning across the table to lightly touch the other girl's hand, 'I have no objection whatsoever in holding off on your wedding arrangements,' she told her seriously. 'Just give me a call when, or if, you decide you do want me to proceed with them. OK?'

Rebecca's cheeks were flushed. 'What do you mean, "if"?'

'I liked your father's house, Rebecca,' Cyn told her lightly, picking up her fork to eat the salad she had ordered as her main course. She could see from Rebecca's expression that she was slightly unsure of this sudden change of subject. But if she would just hear Cyn out, she would see it wasn't a change of subject at all. 'The sitting-room we were in yesterday was very elegant, very restful too—with that magnificent view of the garden.' She forked some of the salad into her mouth, eating it with obvious enjoyment, deliberately not meeting Rebecca's gaze as the truth slowly dawned on the other girl.

'Yes,' Rebecca agreed dazedly, 'it's lovely. I——Oh, God!' she suddenly choked, bending her head so that no one else in the restaurant should see her tears. 'You saw!' she groaned raggedly.

'I saw the young mistress of the house talking to the gardener, that's all,' Cyn assured her gently. 'I just want you to realise that I'm in no hurry to begin making your wedding arrangements for you, but that I'll be happy to help when you do feel more comfortable with them. And the identity of the bridegroom,' she added softly. 'After all, this isn't just about a wedding, is it? There's the rest of your life afterwards to consider.'

Rebecca drew in a shaky breath, her tears firmly under control again now, her shoulders taut as she straightened, picking up her own fork ready to eat. 'Thank you,' she accepted with quiet dignity.

Cyn couldn't help but admire the girl. She liked her! She had never believed she would say that about any woman Wolf had decided to marry, but there was something so vulnerable about Rebecca; she made Cyn feel slightly maternal, she realised disgustedly.

'Let's eat, shall we?' she said more sharply than she had meant to. But how could she possibly feel maternal about Wolf's bride? It was totally ridiculous!

'How did your dinner with Gerald go yesterday?'

Cyn eyed Wolf incredulously, as she sat across the width of his desk from him.

There had been a lot of work for her to catch up on when she returned from her lunch with Rebecca, and she had been totally caught up in the menu for a dinner party she was catering for next week, when the telephone call came through from Wolf's office, and his secretary informed her that Wolf would like to see her, if it wasn't too much trouble.

If it wasn't too much trouble! Wolf and Rebecca both seemed to think she had nothing more to do with her time than run around after the pair of them; they must think she had no other clients other than them! And then she had remembered that Wolf had seen her appointment book yesterday when he wandered about her office, that he must have seen then that she wasn't exactly inundated with appointments for the next few weeks; there was usually a short lull in weddings directly after Easter, picking up again in June. That was still no reason for him to assume she could just drop everything and drive into London to see him!

But his secretary, polite as ever, had firmly told her that no, Mr Thornton wasn't able to drive out to see her, that he was in a meeting at the moment, and didn't expect to be out of it until shortly after five o'clock. Which meant Cyn couldn't even talk to him personally to find out what all this was about! She had tersely informed the woman at the other end of the telephone that she would be in to see Wolf at five-thirty, before ringing off abruptly.

She had then spent the rest of the afternoon totally unable to concentrate on what she was doing, so she might just as well have driven up to see Wolf immediately after the call came in. Except that he was in a meeting and couldn't even see her until after five!

She wished she had never met Gerald Harcourt at that Easter wedding, never heard of his daughter Rebecca, certainly that she had never met Wolf again!

Especially now that it seemed the only reason Wolf had wanted to see her at all was to ask her how her date with Gerald had gone the evening before. It was none of his business, dammit!

She stood up restlessly, the slight heel on her shoes immediately sinking into the deep pile of the cool blue carpet. It seemed that no expense had been spared on the Thornton Industries' head offices, everywhere she had seen being decorated and furnished in the height of luxury.

Cyn hadn't been here in the past, the office not being one of the places Wolf had been interested in going to then, although she had to admit that this harsher, more arrogant Wolf was much more suited to the world of business than to being artistically creative. Although she still couldn't help but feel sad for the loss of that other, more relaxed and teasing Wolf...

This would never do; she brought her wandering thoughts back in check. *This* Wolf was harsh, arrogant, was coldly forceful, and she would do well to remember that!

'What did you want to see me about, Wolf?' she asked briskly, totally ignoring his probing question, her humour not improved after driving into London for the second time today.

He leant back in his leather chair, his eyes narrowed, his three-piece suit a dark navy today, with a stark white shirt and pale blue tie, the dark blond hair brushed severely back from his face, making him look every inch his thirty-five years. Also every inch the successful businessman he obviously now was.

His mouth twisted harshly. 'Not going to answer my question about your date with Gerald?' He gave an acknowledging inclination of his head. 'He's been unusually quiet about it too,' he drawled drily. 'Which can only mean one of two things——'

'You asked Gerald about our date?' Cyn at last managed to gasp, too incredulous at first to be able to say anything.

'—either the two of you being together was a dismal failure never to be repeated,' Wolf continued as if she hadn't just interrupted, 'or the two of you became lovers.' His voice had hardened now, his eyes narrowed. 'In which case Gerald, being the gentleman that he is where the ladies in his life are concerned, wouldn't discuss you with me or anyone else.'

'It's a pity the same can't be said for you!' Cyn snapped heatedly, eyes flashing deeply violet.

Wolf hadn't moved, and yet there was a tension about him now that hadn't been quite so pronounced minutes ago. 'What's that supposed to mean?' His voice was dangerously soft.

She glared across the desk at him. 'Obviously you didn't feel the same compunction about discussing me with him!' she accused. 'Or is it just that you don't consider me a lady?' she challenged defensively. After all, seven years ago she had become Wolf's lover after knowing him only a few days; maybe he believed she had known a string of other lovers since then!

The truth of it was that there had been no other men that close to her since Wolf. Oh, she and Roger had fallen back into the easy relationship they had had before she met Wolf, going out together a couple of times a week, and they still did meet occasionally now, but she hadn't allowed anyone close enough to her for there to even be the possibility of a physical relationship between them; Wolf had been the man she loved, and it hadn't worked out, so instead she gained her happiness vicariously by arranging other people's weddings.

'I didn't *discuss* you with Gerald, at any time,' Wolf's voice was icily controlled as he answered her, 'but in the circumstances, it's a little odd, considering we had a business lunch together today, that he didn't mention seeing you last night.'

Cyn relaxed slightly, although it was a little odd to think that Wolf and Gerald had been lunching together while she and Rebecca were doing the same thing. Thank God they hadn't all decided to lunch at the same restaurant; wouldn't that have made an interesting meeting! 'Maybe having dinner with me was particularly unmemorable for him,' she suggested drily.

Wolf met her gaze steadily. 'I doubt that,' he said quietly.

Cyn looked at him sharply, but his expression remained enigmatic, giving her no insight as to what he might have meant by that remark. She sighed, putting up a hand to her throbbing temple; the strain of driving in London had certainly taken its toll on her today. 'Could you just tell me why I'm here, Wolf, so I can go home, have a soak in the bath, some dinner, and then put my feet up for the rest of the weekend?' After the last two days she felt desperately in need of the rest!

'Hmm, sounds tempting.' He gave a rueful grimace that told her he wouldn't be doing anything as relaxing with his weekend.

Her mouth twisted. 'I'm sure the head of Thornton Industries could do the same thing—if he chose to.'

'Are you?' he sighed. 'I'm not so sure. Although I may be able to find some time to relax this weekend.' He frowned suddenly. 'Now that Rebecca has gone away for a couple of days.'

'I'm sure you—— Rebecca's gone away?' Cyn hoped her voice sounded as innocently curious as she wanted it to!

Rebecca had made no mention about going away when the two of them had talked earlier, so maybe her decision to do so had been a sudden one, so that she could think very carefully before committing herself to a marriage—and a man!—she didn't seem totally sure of? Cyn sincerely hoped so; Rebecca was too young to tie herself to a relationship she wasn't a hundred per cent sure about. Although she doubted if Wolf would see it in quite the same way, especially if it had been anything Cyn had said to the girl that had caused her to rethink the situation!

She could be totally wrong about that, Cyn acknowledged, and maybe Rebecca would come back having realised just how lucky she was to be marrying someone like Wolf, after all. Although there was still the question of that young gardener...

'That's what I wanted to talk to you about,' Wolf nodded abruptly. 'Rebecca has—been under a lot of strain the last few months, with our engagement and other things,' he dismissed briskly. 'So if you have any questions about the wedding arrangements during the next few days, perhaps you could come to me with them?'

Cyn had noticed the young girl's engagement ring, the single large diamond, had guessed by the way she unconsciously sought its presence, twisting it around on her finger, that it was a fairly new acquisition. In which case the wedding must now seem to be absolutely rushing towards her—hence her near-panic, Cyn would guess. Even Rebecca's confused feelings over the gardener might just be part of her pre-wedding nerves too. Cyn was no longer sure whether she wished that were the case or not...

'I don't usually work weekends,' she told Wolf impatiently. 'And you could have said all this on the telephone.' She sighed as she realised that her second trip in here today had been a waste of time, and picked up her handbag in preparation to leave. 'Maybe you have time to waste, Wolf, but I——'

'Sit down!' Wolf ordered thunderously, sitting forward in his chair now to rest his arms on the top of his desk, all pretence of relaxing totally gone. 'I don't have time to waste either,' he rasped harshly. 'I never did,' he added enigmatically.

He used to say that concerning his painting, Cyn remembered painfully. What had happened to that? This office had several originals on its walls, but even a cursory glance told her that none of them were Wolf's own. 'Why don't you paint any more, Wolf?' The question was blurted out before she even had time to think about it. And as Wolf's face darkened ominously, she knew she shouldn't have asked the question at all, let alone as bluntly as she had. But she wanted to know, dammit!

'I've just told you,' he grated coldly, 'I don't have any time to waste!'

Cyn gasped. 'Your painting was never a waste, Wolf!'

His eyes narrowed. 'And what would *you* know about it?'

She paled, swallowing hard. Wolf had never been cruel in the past, but she realised he was a master at it now, that he had meant to be insulting—and that he had succeeded! 'I'd better go——'

'I haven't finished!' he said impatiently. 'We keep being side-tracked by the past. Which is something else I wanted to talk to you about—except not the parts we keep discussing.' He looked grim. 'I realised after I'd left you yesterday and had time to think things over——'

'That you behaved like an overbearing, autocratic pig!' Cyn accused with feeling, recovering slightly from his deliberate taunt; she couldn't allow herself to be destroyed all over again by this man.

His mouth twisted. 'That we hadn't discussed Rebecca not being told of our past—association,' he completed pointedly. 'Of course she knows I was engaged to someone else seven years ago——'

'Big of you to have told her even that,' Cyn snapped, resentful of this whole conversation; as if she had any wish for Rebecca, or anyone else, to realise she had once been going to marry Wolf herself!

Wolf's eyes narrowed to icy-cold slits. 'It would have been pointless to have kept that from her,' he bit out tersely. 'But I saw no reason to bore her with the details.'

'Of course not,' Cyn scorned, stung by his attitude. 'Although you didn't really have to tell her anything; there were so few people who even knew we were engaged at all!'

'And whose fault was that?' Wolf accused harshly.

Hers, she freely admitted that. But although she had been sure of her love for Wolf, she had still been insecure about his wealthy background, even if he did choose to dismiss it most of the time. He was still a Thornton, had known a much more privileged childhood than her, had never known what it was like to want something so badly that when it actually came to her she had been terrified of losing it. Wolf's love had been like that to her. And, in retrospect, she had been wise to step warily where any kind of permanent future for them was concerned. Because it just hadn't happened.

'This is all past history, Wolf,' she sighed wearily.

'I couldn't agree more,' he nodded abruptly. 'And I want it to remain that way,' he added warningly.

'Consider it forgotten,' Cyn told him resentfully, knowing she would never forget it. And from the thunderous expression on Wolf's face, neither would he— but for different reasons, Cyn didn't doubt! 'Now I——' She broke off abruptly as the door behind her suddenly opened; most of the staff had been leaving the building as she arrived at five-thirty, and Wolf had dismissed his efficient secretary once she had shown Cyn into his office, so who was this walking unannounced into Wolf's office in this familiar——?

Cyn only needed one glance across the office to know exactly who would dare to do such a thing.

Barbara!

It might have been almost seven years since she had last seen the other woman, but Cyn would know the beautiful Barbara Thornton anywhere. Besides, the other woman had changed little; her hair was still an ebony cloud, although styled shorter than it used to be, her beautifully perfect features still as glowingly youthful, despite the fact that she had to be thirty-three now. And she still wore her clothes, a tailored black dress this evening, with all the style and elegance she had learnt during her years as a top-class model. Yes, Cyn would know the beautiful Barbara Thornton. Anywhere.

'Sorry, Wolf,' the other woman drawled without any sign of real apology in her voice. 'I didn't realise you had someone with you.' She gave Cyn a bright, meaningless smile—a smile that told Cyn, at least, that this woman wouldn't have acted any differently if she had realised Wolf wasn't alone, that she felt perfectly within her rights to walk in on him unannounced in his office. As Alex Thornton's *widow*, Barbara had inherited Alex's shares of Thornton Industries at the time of his death seven years ago, so she was probably right about that!

But as Cyn knew only too well, Barbara had never needed those shares to feel this peremptory right in Wolf's life!

Barbara turned back to Wolf now. 'I just wanted to remind you that dinner—is at eight——' She broke off suddenly, turning sharply back to Cyn, her breath sharply indrawn as she looked at her more closely. 'You!' she accused, green eyes wide with recognition.

There had never been any love lost between the two women. Barbara had treated Cyn, at best, with cool condescension after Wolf had introduced them seven years ago.

Cyn hadn't been too troubled by the other woman's attitude at the time; she had known from the first that Wolf's family wouldn't exactly welcome her with open arms, that she was far from an ideal choice, in the haughty Thornton family's eyes, as the wife of one of the Thornton heirs. After all, she worked as a receptionist in one of their hotels, and her family background was nonexistent, as was her social standing; it was only natural, Cyn had accepted, that they should treat her with a certain amount of wariness until she had shown them that it was Wolf she loved and not his money. Wolf hadn't given a damn what his family thought; he had told them he was marrying her, and that was exactly what he intended doing, whether they approved of her or not!

Only Barbara Thornton's antagonism towards Cyn had had nothing to do with approving or disapproving of her; she had hated her on sight. And from the way she was looking at Cyn now, that feeling had never changed!

But Cyn was seven years older now, she inwardly chided herself as she briefly experienced those familiar feelings of inadequacy where this woman was concerned; she was a successful businesswoman in her own right, even if it was on a much smaller scale than the Thornton company.

She met the other woman's gaze steadily, knowing that, if Barbara appeared not to have changed, then she at least had; never again would she allow herself to be cowed by any member of this powerful family. Besides, she had had the advantage of realising for a couple of days that a meeting like this, when Wolf married Rebecca, was inevitable. She hadn't liked the idea, but she had known that it had to happen. Barbara, in the meantime, still looked completely stunned to see her again after all this time.

'Barbara,' she greeted her drily. 'You're looking well,' she added lightly.

'I'm——!' Barbara broke off, incredulous at Cyn's cool command, and turned those flashing green eyes on Wolf now. 'You didn't tell me you and Lucynda had met again.' She had difficulty controlling the sharp, almost shrill edge to her voice as she tried not to sound accusing.

Barbara, and Wolf's mother Claudia, had both persisted in using her full first name once they had learnt that was what Cyn was short for, both of them claiming to dislike diminutives of names, especially ones as ridiculous as Cyn! Wolf hadn't liked them calling her Lucynda at all, but at the time Cyn hadn't thought it was worth causing an argument over, although she had winced every time they called her Lucynda; it reminded her too much of her years in the orphanage.

How naïvely trusting she had been seven years ago; now she could see the other women's behaviour for exactly what it was, yet another way of the two powerful Thornton women keeping her at a distance from them, and firmly in her place, of letting her know she would never be accepted as one of them.

'My name is Cyn. Or Miss Smith,' she told the other woman before turning back to Wolf—a Wolf who sat watching the two of them with narrowed eyes; probably waiting to see if they scratched each other's eyes out, Cyn acknowledged angrily. She wouldn't give Barbara, or Wolf, the satisfaction! 'I think that's our business concluded for today,' she said coolly, knowing by the way his mouth tightened and his eyes narrowed ominously that he didn't like the way she was talking to him at all. Tough!

'Business?' Barbara echoed sharply. 'What on earth sort of business could the two of you——?'

'I really do have to go,' Cyn cut in, impatient with the way this family assumed she had nothing else to do this evening but stand here listening to them. 'I have a date—with my bath,' she added pointedly as she saw Wolf's eyes narrow questioningly. 'It was—interesting, meeting you again, Barbara,' she told the other woman drily. Barbara was still looking slightly dazed from the encounter.

'Interesting?' the other woman echoed incredulously. 'Wolf, I don't——'

''Bye!' Cyn called lightly as she left the office without haste—only to find herself brought to a sudden halt as familiar fingers grasped tightly about her arm. 'What do you want now, Wolf?' she asked wearily as she turned to face him in the corridor, all the time aware of Barbara waiting inside his office for him.

He looked intently down at her pale face. 'Will you have dinner with me tonight?' he asked gruffly.

Cyn's eyes widened. 'But I thought Barbara just said the two of you were having dinner together?' she frowned.

'We only made the arrangement an hour ago,' Wolf shrugged dismissively. 'I don't have to go.'

He had only learnt late this afternoon that his fiancée was going to be out of town for a couple of days! But immediately he and Barbara had made plans of their own. Nothing had changed, it seemed!

'I wouldn't have dinner with you if I were starving to death!' Cyn told him scornfully, pulling roughly out of his grasp; God, she was going to be covered in bruises at this rate! 'Go back to Barbara,' she advised disgustedly. 'The two of you obviously deserve each other!'

'Cyn——'

'Leave—me—alone, Wolf!' The tone of her voice must have warned him she was close to doing some physical damage of her own if he didn't, because he stepped back from her abruptly—although she was aware of him watching her as she strode forcefully down the corridor to the lift, viciously jabbing at the button, stepping inside the plush lift once the doors had glided open, her violet gaze clashing with his golden one before the doors silently closed again and she began her smooth descent to the ground floor.

Cyn only wished her thoughts were as smoothly untroubled!

She couldn't believe Wolf and Barbara, just *couldn't believe* the two of them!

Seven years ago Cyn had been left in no doubt of the fact that Wolf and Barbara were having an affair, that they had been doing so since the early days of Barbara's marriage to Alex. Just as she didn't doubt now, in spite of Wolf's engagement to Rebecca—an engagement that seemed to be founded on business on Wolf's side rather than love!—that they were still having an affair.

If she only knew where Rebecca had gone for the weekend, she would go and see her and tell her how right she was to feel unsure about marrying Wolf, that she should give him his damned ring back and tell him to go to hell!

As Cyn had...

CHAPTER FIVE

'*I* WANT to know exactly what *you* know about Rebecca going away!'

Cyn drew in a slow controlling breath as Wolf verbally attacked her as soon as she opened her cottage door to his knock. She had been expecting something like this all day, ever since her peaceful Saturday had been shattered at ten o'clock this morning when she received a telephone call from Rebecca Harcourt... She wished, and not for the first time, that she hadn't had her home telephone number as well as her business one printed on the card she had given Rebecca at their first meeting, then she wouldn't have Wolf standing on her doorstep glowering down at her!

'You'd better come in,' she invited him wearily now, stepping back to allow him entrance.

'I—— My God!' he muttered impatiently as he followed her inside the cottage—and almost hit his head on the low-beamed ceiling. 'I didn't realise you lived in the original Seven Dwarfs' cottage!' he rasped insultingly as he lowered his head to avoid another beam.

The height and small size of the rooms was one of the reasons Cyn had been able to rent the cottage in the first place; there weren't too many people short enough to feel comfortable living here! It certainly wasn't suitable for one of the commuter couples who would usually have snapped it up; not too many men must relish the idea of going around permanently bent over in order to be able to walk about their own home!

Wolf looked particularly ridiculous, his size and height making him look more like a giant who *had* stumbled into the Seven Dwarfs' cottage than anything else. Not that many men had been to the cottage at all, and Wolf certainly hadn't been invited here, so it was his own fault if he was now uncomfortable.

He sat down abruptly in one of the armchairs, the cane-based chair creaking under his weight; even the furniture had had to be chosen to fit in with the small proportions of the rooms.

He glared up at Cyn. 'Well?' he barked harshly.

Cyn looked down at him, having none of the problems with the size of the cottage that he obviously did. He was dressed as casually as she was today, both of them wearing denims, Cyn's topped with a bright pink sweatshirt, Wolf wearing a pale cream sweater. But the casualness of their clothes was the only thing they had in common. Wolf's expression was grim, Cyn's deliberately enquiring. She knew what he was talking about, of course she did, but she didn't know how to answer him, had no idea exactly how much he knew concerning Rebecca . . .

'I was just about to make a cup of coffee,' she said lightly. 'Would you like one?'

'No, I damn——' Wolf broke off abruptly, drawing in a slow controlling breath as he sat forward in the chair. 'I didn't come here for coffee, Cyn,' he bit out harshly. 'I came for some answers. Gerald tells me that this morning you received a telephone call from Rebecca asking you to inform him that he isn't to worry about her because she's fine, but that she may stay away longer than the couple of days she initially planned—and that the wedding is off!'

Cyn had still been half asleep when she answered the ringing of her telephone early this morning, having spent a restless night, still churned up over that meeting with Wolf and Barbara in his office. But she had come awake instantly when Rebecca identified herself on the telephone. However, Rebecca hadn't wanted Cyn to talk, had only wanted her to listen, and then pass the message on to her father. When Cyn had protested at the message she wanted her to pass on Rebecca had put the receiver down at the other end.

Cyn had been stunned. What was she supposed to do now? One thing she had known—Rebecca had no intention of telephoning her father and talking to him herself, so if she didn't call him herself he would be left wondering what had happened at the end of the weekend when Rebecca didn't return home from the schoolfriend's she had told him she was visiting. And when Gerald telephoned that friend he would discover that Rebecca hadn't been there at all!

Cyn hadn't liked the position she had been put in at all, and wished once again that she had never heard of the Harcourt family. But as she *had* heard of them, and Rebecca *had* entrusted her with the task of talking to her father, Cyn had had no choice in the end but to telephone Gerald. He had been stunned by what she had to tell him, and wanted to know where Rebecca really was, but as Cyn had no idea...

It hadn't taken Wolf long after Gerald must have spoken to him to decide that Cyn must know more than she was telling them.

She shrugged. 'That was exactly what Rebecca told me to tell her father.' She grimaced at the inadequacy of it. But Rebecca had been adamant that she had nothing else to say on the matter, so what else could Cyn possibly say about it?

'Why you, Cyn?' Wolf's eyes were narrowed up at her speculatively. 'Why did Rebecca choose you to talk to rather than one of us? After all, Gerald is her father, and I'm—I was—her fiancé,' he amended grimly.

Cyn swallowed hard. 'Possibly that's the reason she chose me,' she suggested lightly. 'The two of you were too close, whereas I——'

'Yes?' Wolf prompted as she hesitated.

'I don't know why she chose me either, Wolf,' Cyn snapped, her eyes flashing deeply violet. 'You'll have to ask Rebecca that, won't you!'

'But I can't, because *she* isn't here,' he reminded her softly. '*You* are.'

And she wished she weren't! She had known there was going to be trouble over Rebecca's behaviour, had tried to think of some answers she could give Wolf—because she had known he would come here demanding some!— but the truth of the matter was that she just didn't have any to give him. Not without betraying Rebecca's trust in her. And she couldn't—wouldn't do that.

She shrugged. 'And I've told you everything Rebecca told me to.'

Wolf still watched her with narrowed eyes. 'Everything?' he echoed silkily.

She couldn't quite meet his gaze now. Yes, she had told them everything Rebecca had told her to tell her father and Wolf—but not everything she knew! And Wolf was astute enough to realise that, if Gerald wasn't.

Rebecca hadn't answered her when Cyn had asked if she was doing this thinking she needed to be alone, had just repeated the message she wanted Cyn to give her father. But Cyn would be very interested to know if the young golden god of a gardener arrived for work on Monday morning...

'Everything,' Cyn repeated firmly. 'There's really nothing more I can tell you, Wolf, so if you wouldn't mind, I——'

'But I do mind, Cyn,' he told her evenly as he once again stood up—and instantly cursed the low ceiling once again as he ducked to avoid hitting his head. 'I wanted to talk to you about last night.'

She was discovering that the tiny rooms in the cottage had another disadvantage besides the obvious ones; the small proportions made Wolf seem very close, very dominating with his superior height—and more than a little dangerous! What was it they said, the best form of defence was attack? Well then, she had better attack, and quickly, because her defences were starting to crumble!

'Your fiancée has just called off your wedding, and *you* want to talk to *me*?' she scorned incredulously. 'I think it's Rebecca you should be trying to talk to!'

He shook his head. 'I don't happen to know where she is, do I? But I do know where you are,' he added with satisfaction.

Cyn swallowed hard. 'I have nothing more to say about last night. In fact, now that the wedding appears to have been cancelled,' she continued more confidently—she would *not* talk about Barbara, would not put herself through that emotional torture a second time! 'I can't see any reason for us to have any further contact at all. Unless, of course, Rebecca changes her mind about the wedding, in which case I'll be more than happy to talk to both of you concerning the—Wolf!' she croaked as he reached out suddenly and pulled her up hard against his chest, the expression on his face grimly determined, to say the least.

'Shut up, woman!' he rasped. 'Just shut up,' he groaned before his head lowered and his mouth claimed hers.

Cyn wished he would stop doing this, because there was no way she could resist him. She had once loved this man—— Once? God, she still loved him, she realised with a sickening jolt in her stomach. How could that be? How could she still love this man, a man who had not only betrayed *her*, but also the girl he had been about to marry in a few months' time?

She didn't know how she did, she just knew, as her body and senses responded to his caresses, that she had never stopped loving him. In spite of it all, she loved him! He was the reason she had never been able to feel any emotion stronger than liking for any other man.

She pulled away from him with a choked sob. 'Stop it, Wolf,' she told him shakily, pushing at his chest. 'I don't want this.'

'I *need* this!' he claimed determinedly, his head lowering to hers once again.

She was too weakened by his closeness to protest this time when his mouth claimed hers, his lips sipping and tasting, his tongue dipping and caressing, and her arms moved up about his neck as she pulled him down to her.

It had always been like this between them, this wild racing of pulses, this wild cry of every nerve-ending for the caresses that would drive them towards the edge of fulfilment.

Wolf was filled with the same sense of urgency as his hands roamed restlessly over her body and the kiss deepened and lengthened, the pulsing of his thighs telling her of that need he had claimed only minutes earlier.

God, how she loved the feel of his hair beneath her fingertips, those fingers becoming entwined in the long silky blondness as she held him against her, the tip of her tongue meeting the quest of his in answering longing.

What was she doing? What was *Wolf* doing? This was wrong, so very wrong, for both of them! It hadn't worked out between them seven years ago, wouldn't work out now either, and Cyn knew she had no intention of becoming just another conquest to Wolf. And she could never be anything else. Had never been anything else, not really—— Was that why he was doing this, because she had been the one to end things between them all those years ago? God, she was so stupid...!

She wrenched away from him, his fingers biting painfully into her arms preventing her from moving away from him completely, his expression slightly dazed as he looked down at her questioningly; and no wonder, for seconds ago she had been pliantly aroused in his arms!

'What's the matter, Wolf?' she said scornfully. 'Can't you be without a woman in your life for more than a couple of hours?'

He blinked, his brain still slightly fogged by the passion they had shared only seconds ago. 'What——?'

'Your fiancée had gone away for the weekend last night, so you invited not one woman but two to join you for dinner!' Cyn accused disgustedly. 'Now today, when it seems Rebecca's panicked completely and called off the wedding, you don't go chasing after her claiming your undying love for her and trying to convince her the two of you do have a future together—oh, no, you come to *my* cottage and try to make love to *me*. It seems to me Rebecca's had a lucky escape!' As *she* had, she told herself angrily.

Wolf's hands dropped away from her arms as if he had been burned, the dazed expression replaced by chilling anger as he listened to her scathing words.

But Cyn was beyond caring about how he felt about what she was saying. This anger wasn't only for Rebecca, but for herself too, for all the past pain Wolf had given her, and all the heartache she knew was yet to come; getting over Wolf this time was going to be much harder than it had been the first time!

'Now get out of here, Wolf,' she told him with steady dignity. 'Get out, and stay out!'

'You're twisting things round to suit what you want to believe,' he rasped harshly, his mouth a taut line, his jaw tightly clenched.

'I *want* to believe you're going out of that door!' Her eyes flashed deeply violet.

'Cyn——'

'Why don't you ask yourself why I want to believe those things, Wolf?' she challenged, her eyes over-bright with unshed tears; she would not cry in front of him, she wouldn't! 'It's because I don't want you here. I'll never want you here. I don't want *you*!' The last came out slightly shrill as she willed him to go away, knowing she didn't have the physical strength or ability to actually make him go if he chose not to. But why should he want to stay somewhere he so obviously wasn't wanted?

His eyes glittered ominously, his face looking as if it were etched from granite at that moment. 'We have to talk——'

'We have nothing to say to each other,' she snapped tautly. 'Go and cry on some other woman's shoulder!' Barbara's. She had always been more than willing to listen to his problems. And anything else he chose to tell her.

Wolf's mouth tightened. 'As you've already pointed out, I'm hardly in a desperate state about the wedding being called off,' he rasped grimly. 'And that's because——'

'You didn't love her!' Cyn finished accusingly. 'I already knew that. You're incapable of loving anyone! That's why I——' She broke off as she realised she had been about to admit to having encouraged Rebecca to think very seriously before she committed herself to a marriage she wasn't sure of; that would be all the ammunition Wolf needed to rip her to pieces!

'Yes?' Wolf prompted, silkily soft.

Her cheeks were no longer pale now but darkly flushed. 'Why *I* didn't marry you myself seven years ago!' she substituted defiantly, knowing by the icy glitter to his eyes now that he was absolutely furious. Well, so was she, dammit, furious at the way he had thought he could just walk back into her life—and her bed!

'All right, Cyn,' he ground out harshly, a nerve pulsing in his rigidly clenched jaw, 'I'll go. But if I ever find out you were instrumental in Rebecca's sudden flight I'll——'

Cyn never found out exactly what he would do to her if he realised she had spoken to Rebecca—although she could surely guess!—because at that moment he turned with forceful strides towards the door, obviously forgetting the low height of the ceiling, as he cracked his head on one of the beams, while at the same time seeming to catch his foot on something too as he went sprawling across the room, narrowly missing hitting his head again, this time on the dresser that stood against the far wall.

It was all over in a matter of seconds, and Cyn could only stand by helplessly as she watched the series of events, totally baffled as to what had actually happened—although she moved quickly enough once she realised Wolf wasn't about to get immediately back up on to his feet.

He lay on the carpet lengthways across the room, and part of her marvelled at the fact that he had actually managed to avoid crashing into any of the furniture, the small two-seater sofa behind him, the coffee-table in front of him. Not that she thought he was going to be in the least grateful for that—when, or if, he got up.

Cyn quickly moved the coffee-table out of the way, going down on her knees beside Wolf. His eyes were closed, and he still wasn't moving. Oh, God, he hadn't been knocked out, had he? What were you supposed to do with someone who was knocked out? Perhaps she should telephone for an ambulance? For a doctor, at least?

But when she picked up the receiver to dial the emergency number it was to discover the line was dead. And no amount of pressing down on the connection made any difference to that eerie silence.

'You're wasting your time with that; it's what I tripped over!'

The harshness of Wolf's voice in the otherwise silent room almost made Cyn drop the receiver and fall over herself. She turned to him with wide eyes, relieved to see he was now sitting up, at least. But from the grim expression on his face, *he* couldn't see anything to feel relieved about!

She put down the useless receiver. 'How are you feeling?'

'How——!' He drew in a controlling breath, shooting her an impatient glare. 'How the hell do you think I'm feeling, with half a mile of telephone line wrapped around my ankle!'

That was when Cyn saw what he had meant by his first remark; her telephone line wasn't just wrapped around his ankle, he had actually ripped the socket out of the wall. No wonder the line had been dead just now. So much for calling him a doctor!

'I was trying to get help for you—I don't think you should move until a doctor has looked at you,' she told him quickly as he seemed to be trying to get to his feet. Trying, because he didn't seem to be doing a very good job of it; he was obviously in pain somewhere as he gave a low groan. 'You were only unconscious for a few moments,' she acknowledged as she put her hand on his shoulder to stop him from moving any further. 'But it was long enough to——'

'I wasn't unconscious at all, Cyn,' Wolf rasped, the expression in his eyes no longer just impatient; the furious glitter was back in the golden depths. 'I was lying down here with my eyes closed counting up to a hundred so that I didn't immediately strangle you for the fact that you always did like a mile of telephone line so that you could move from room to room while you talked on the telephone!'

She moved back as if she had been stung, colour darkening her cheeks as she remembered the fact—as Wolf obviously did too!—that seven years ago he had had to call in an engineer to his apartment to put in a longer telephone line after she had 'moved from room to room as she talked on the telephone' and pulled the wire from the socket several times and disconnected her calls. It was disconcerting to realise this man knew her so well...

'Obviously you only need *half* a mile of extra line in this doll's house,' Wolf continued disgustedly, having managed to untangle the line from his leg now, and impatiently throwing it to one side. 'But it's still enough for me to have almost broken my neck on it!'

Cyn didn't think now was the time to tell him that this was a cottage, that they were supposed to be small. Character, the estate agent's blurb had called it, and she happened to like it exactly as it was.

All of which was totally irrelevant to what had just happened, she accepted ruefully. If it had been anyone else but Wolf...!

But of course it wouldn't have been—would it?—not the way her luck had been going lately. If things had been going her way at all at the moment Wolf wouldn't have turned out to be Rebecca Harcourt's fiancé in the first place, and then she wouldn't have met him again at all.

Not that that was really relevant either; she *had* met him again, and he was now prostrate on her sitting-room floor—apparently unable to get up again, she realised with horror, as he attempted to move and could only give that pained groan once again.

Cyn was on her knees beside him, looking him over worriedly; it seemed as if they were going to need a doctor after all. 'Where does it hurt?' she frowned. 'Is it your head?'

'My head just has a lump on it—the size of an egg!' he muttered with a pained wince after he had put up a hand to the side of his head and discovered the lump there. 'But maybe that will have knocked some sense into me—at last!' he grated, glaring at her once again.

EXCLUSIVE PRIZE# 6N 761490

BIG BUCKS

	$			

HURRY!
This Jackpot must be claimed!

Scratch Here ↗

LUCKY CHARM GAME!

Claim
4 FREE Books
AND a FREE
Mystery Gift!

YES! I have played my BIG BUCKS game card as instructed. Enter my Big Bucks Prize number in the MILLION DOLLAR Sweepstakes III and also enter me for the Extra Bonus Prize. When winners are selected, tell me if I've won. If the Lucky Charm is scratched off, I will also receive everything revealed, as explained on the back and on the opposite page.

306 CIH AQTR
(C-H-P-08/94)

NAME _____

ADDRESS _____ APT. _____

CITY _____ PROV. _____ POSTAL CODE _____

NO PURCHASE OR OBLIGATION NECESSARY TO ENTER SWEEPSTAKES.

© 1993 HARLEQUIN ENTERPRISES LTD.   PRINTED IN U.S.A.

TWO WAYS TO WIN BIG BUCKS!

1. Uncover 5 $ signs in a row. . . . BINGO! You're eligible to win the $1,000,000.00 SWEEPSTAKES!

2. Uncover 5 $ signs in a row AND uncover $ signs in all 4 corners . . . BINGO! You're also eligible for the $50,000.00 EXTRA BONUS PRIZE!

THE HARLEQUIN READER SERVICE®: HERE'S HOW IT WORKS

Accepting free books places you under no obligation to buy anything. You may keep the books and gift and return the shipping statement marked "cancel". If you do not cancel, about a month later we will send you 6 additional novels and bill you just $2.74 each plus 25¢ delivery and GST*. That's the complete price, and – compared to cover prices of $3.50 each – quite a bargain! You may cancel at any time, but if you choose to continue, every month we'll send you 6 more books, which you may either purchase at the discount price...or return at our expense and cancel your subscription.

*Terms and prices subject to change without notice. Canadian residents add applicable provincial taxes and GST.

019561919-L2A5X3-BR01

"BIG BUCKS"
MILLION DOLLAR SWEEPSTAKES III
P.O. BOX 609
FORT ERIE, ONTARIO
L2A 9Z9

Canada Post Corporation / Société canadienne des postes

Postage paid | Port payé
if mailed in Canada | si posté au Canada

Business Reply | Réponse d'affaires

MAIL⇒POSTE

019561919   01

'It's my ankle that seems to be preventing me from getting up.' He shook his head with self-disgust at his inability to be able to do such a simple thing as get to his feet.

Cyn looked down at the injured ankle, inconsequentially noting as she did so that both Wolf's socks were black; obviously he was no longer ever so distracted that he put on odd socks. She knew it was a stupid thing for her to have even noticed, but it was nevertheless yet another indication that this man wasn't the Wolf she had known in the past; unless she had been there to remind him, *that* Wolf had often—as he had told her at their very first meeting that he did—gone out with odd socks on.

'I solved that particular problem by buying all black socks,' Wolf spoke gruffly as he obviously guessed her thoughts.

She gave him a sharp look, quickly looking away again at the rueful humour she saw in his eyes. 'I'm sure that's more sensible, with all those dark business suits you wear,' she dismissed abruptly. The Wolf of the past had never been sensible. But then that Wolf hadn't worn business suits either, would have dismissed any suggestion that he should do so.

Once again Cyn wondered what had happened to him during the last seven years. And she refused to believe, no matter what he had said to the contrary, that it had anything to do with her; nothing she could have done would ever have turned him into a businessman. And she wouldn't have wanted it to. She had been proud of his painting, so sure he was going to succeed.

'I wish all my problems could have been solved as easily,' Wolf added grimly now. 'Cyn——'

'Let's see if we can get you moved,' she said briskly, standing up to bend down and put her hand under his arm. 'If not, with the telephone being out of action, I'll have to drive to the doctor's and get him to come out here to you.'

Wolf made no attempt to move, but sat looking up at her, so close she could see the black flecks in the gold of his eyes. 'End of conversation?' he prompted gruffly.

Cyn refused to meet his gaze. 'The past is best forgotten, Wolf,' she told him offhandedly.

His hand moved out to grasp her arm. 'I'm not talking about the past——'

'Well, don't fool yourself into thinking there's a now!' she bit out scornfully. 'The only here and now we have is your injured ankle—and I intend getting professional help for that as soon as possible,' she said briskly, deliberately moving so that his hand fell from her arm. 'Can you try to at least get into a chair so that I can take a better look at your ankle?' It was cramped, to say the least, sandwiched as he was between the sofa and the coffee-table.

He continued to look up at her for long, tension-filled minutes, then he nodded slowly, his expression grim at the effort it took for him to move at all; the ankle was obviously very painful indeed.

In fact, when Cyn finally looked at it once he was in the chair, she wondered how he had managed not to shout out loud at the pain moving must have caused him. His ankle was swollen to twice its normal size, and she knew if she didn't soon get his shoe off it would have to be cut from him. Which would be a pity, as the shoes were obviously handmade, and very expensive.

Yet another indication of the wealthy businessman lifestyle Wolf now enjoyed.

Not that his clothes hadn't been of good quality in the past, they had been; it was just that he hadn't seemed to particularly care what he wore. Now his clothes, as with everything else about him, seemed to have been chosen with studied care. Unless he hadn't chosen them! Barbara was still very prominent in his life, and Cyn had never forgotten the fact that the other woman had decorated his flat for him all those years ago. For the times the two of them could be together...?

Cyn didn't want to think about that, it was still all too painful.

'The shoe will have to come off,' she told him abruptly, lifting his foot up on to her knee. 'Sorry,' she muttered as he gave a pained groan at her rough treatment, moving more cautiously now as she unlaced the shoe and gently eased it loose so that it no longer pressed down into his swollen foot. Slipping the loosened shoe off obviously caused him further pain, although he didn't actually say that it did, the grim set of his face telling its own story. 'Why don't you just scream and shout like other people when they're in pain?' she snapped, impatient with his stoic attitude; why couldn't he just be *normal*, for a change!

'Will that change anything?' he said quietly.

She looked up at him sharply, quickly looking away again as she saw the pain etched into his features. 'I'm sorry,' she sighed at her own lack of feeling, sitting back on her heels. 'I think you may have to go to the hospital.' She frowned at the amount of damage he appeared to have done to his ankle; he might even have broken it.

'I've known that for some time,' he nodded. 'The question is, will you drive me there?'

'Will I——? Of course I'll drive you there!' She glared at him for even thinking she might not. *She* hadn't changed that much. 'I hate to see anyone in pain,' she snapped dismissively.

'That's me firmly put in my place,' Wolf drawled with a grimace. 'Just in case I should have thought your concern was personal,' he added ruefully at her questioning look.

Cyn didn't even bother to answer him, concentrating all her attention on getting him outside to her van so that she could drive him to the West Middlesex Hospital, about five miles away—which proved difficult in itself. Wolf was unable to put any weight on his injured ankle at all; his arm was about her shoulders as he leaned heavily on her on the slow walk—hobble!—out to her van parked in the driveway.

'I think you'll be more comfortable in the back,' she frowned as she realised he couldn't possibly climb up into the passenger-seat in the driving compartment, but that he would probably be able to fall into the back of the van without too much trouble.

Which was exactly what he did, almost taking her with him as she wasn't strong enough to stop him overbalancing!

Cyn felt hot and irritated when she finally had him settled into the back of the van, not least, she admitted, because of all the physical contact necessary with Wolf to get him there. No matter how she might try to convince herself that she and Wolf were totally wrong for each other, her body seemed to have other ideas, and even now she could feel her nipples taut beneath her pink sweatshirt; thank God the material wasn't such that Wolf was aware of them too!

'You'll have to move my car, I'm afraid.' He grimaced at the BMW parked directly behind the van.

'Well, I didn't intend reversing over it!' She glared at him for the unnecessary reminder; she was well aware of the fact that she would have to move his car. She was also aware that she would rather not have done so in the small confines of the driveway. It would be just her luck to back the expensive car into her garden wall!

Knowing Wolf was sitting watching her, with the van doors still open, didn't help. But finally, with a grating of gears—and more than a little cursing!—Cyn managed to manoeuvre Wolf's car out of the way enough to be able to reverse the van down the driveway and out on to the lane.

She deliberately didn't think about him sitting in the back as she drove to the hospital; she dared not allow herself to dwell on the pain the jolting of the van must be giving his ankle, just concentrated on her driving.

And once they reached the hospital the experienced staff took over, two able-bodied ambulancemen helping him out of the van into a waiting wheelchair, a nurse taking him off to an examination-room, leaving Cyn in the waiting-room feeling more than a little superfluous.

It seemed she was waiting there forever, and she began to wonder if they hadn't all forgotten about her completely; the rumblings of her stomach told her it was suffering for the lunch she had missed earlier through Wolf's arrival. At this rate she was going to miss dinner too!

But finally Wolf was wheeled back into the waiting-room, his ankle noticeably bandaged but, fortunately, not in plaster, which must mean he hadn't actually broken any bones—although his face looked grimmer than ever, and Cyn could only guess at the pain the examination and following treatment had given him.

'Nothing broken,' the nurse announced cheerfully as she brought the wheelchair to a halt beside Cyn. 'Although your husband will need these to get about on for a while.' She produced a pair of crutches. 'Although not too much of that for the first couple of days, Mr Thornton; you need to rest that ankle until the swelling goes down,' she told Wolf sternly before going off to deal with the next patient.

Cyn stood up, looking down wordlessly at Wolf, deliberately ignoring the natural mistake the young nurse had made in assuming Wolf was her husband because she had driven him to the hospital, much as she had felt her cheeks burn at the error. Not that Wolf seemed in the least perturbed by the mistake, so why should she?

What did they do now? Obviously Wolf's injury wasn't serious enough for him to be admitted to hospital, but at the same time he couldn't go back to his flat alone either. And yet the thought of having to drive him to his mother's house, of possibly having to see the other woman again—worse, having to see Barbara again!—filled her with dread.

But she needn't have worried; Wolf seemed to have his own answer to that problem!

'You'll have to take me back to your cottage for a few days, of course,' he announced dismissively.

As far as Cyn was concerned there was no 'of course' about it; he couldn't possibly stay at her cottage with her, for any length of time!

CHAPTER SIX

'I DON'T have anywhere else to go,' Wolf told Cyn once they were back in the van. He was in the driving compartment beside her this time, having managed, with the aid of the crutches, to lever himself up there, the crutches now relegated to the back.

From anyone else a statement like this might have produced a sympathetic, even pitying response from Cyn. And it might have been totally deserved—if it were anyone else but Wolf. But she knew it was totally untrue; there were any number of places he could go to be looked after besides her cottage.

'You'll have to move,' he told her now mildly after glancing in the side-mirror. 'There's an ambulance trying to get parked behind us.'

Cyn had brought the van up outside the accident department so that it wasn't so far for Wolf to go, and she saw, after a brief glimpse in her own mirror, that he was right about the ambulance. 'OK, I'll move the van,' she told him grimly as she put the vehicle into gear. 'But I am not driving you back to my cottage!' she added forcefully.

She moved the van only a short distance away to the car park before parking there, turning in her seat to look at Wolf. He returned her gaze blandly now.

'I mean it, Wolf,' she told him tightly, unnerved by his calmness. 'You are not coming back to my cottage with me. I— I'll drive you to your mother's house, if you want to go there,' she offered with obvious reluctance. But even seeing Claudia and Barbara again was preferable to having Wolf at her cottage with her!

His mouth twisted as he obviously guessed her thoughts. 'That's very generous of you,' he drawled. 'And believe me, I know just how generous; you never did get along with my mother!'

'I got along with her just fine,' Cyn contradicted heatedly. 'She just didn't like me.'

'Was that any reason——? Never mind,' he rasped at Cyn's stubbornly unresponsive expression. 'It would upset my mother to see me like this,' he stated firmly.

From what she remembered of Claudia Thornton the other woman would enjoy nothing better than having Wolf in her manipulative clutches virtually immobile, and, as such, powerless to stop her machinations. Unless Claudia had changed—which Cyn very much doubted!

'She never really recovered from the stroke she had after Alex's death,' Wolf continued grimly at Cyn's sceptical expression. 'She's had several minor ones since then. Another major one might kill her. And her initial response to seeing me like this might just cause one,' he added decisively.

Cyn hadn't even known of the first one. She couldn't imagine Claudia as being anything else but completely in command, of herself, and of her family. Short, her figure petite to say the least, Claudia gave the impression of delicacy—a totally misleading impression, as Cyn had found to her cost.

Claudia hadn't approved of Cyn for Wolf, although she had always been careful not to show that disapproval too strongly in front of him, making Cyn's own wariness of the older woman all the more noticeable, a fact that Wolf had commented on more than once when they were alone. But she hadn't been able to control the way she felt about his mother, just as she was sure Claudia hadn't been able to change the way she felt about her either!

'I'm sorry,' Cyn said abruptly. 'I didn't realise.'

'Why should you?' Wolf dismissed coldly. 'You just wanted out of my life. The absolute bloody hell I was going through didn't—— Forget it,' he bit out abruptly, shaking his head. 'As you've said, the past is the past, and raking it up isn't going to solve anything now.'

But it was evident to Cyn just how much it still disturbed him, because Wolf only swore when he was upset about something. Perhaps now wasn't the time either to point out that he could always go to Barbara ... !

But the other woman wasn't the past; from what Cyn had seen the other night, Barbara was still very much in the present tense for Wolf. Cyn straightened defensively; she couldn't help it, just thinking of Barbara Thornton, and the part she had played in her past unhappiness, was enough to make her hackles rise, even now.

'Barbara, then,' she said sharply. 'I'm sure she would be pleased to have you stay with her.' Her mouth twisted scornfully as she thought of just how much the other woman would like that.

'Barbara moved into Thornton House with my mother after Alex's death, and she's stayed there ever since,' Wolf bit out curtly, straightening in his seat. 'But as it's obvious you would rather I went anywhere else but with you, perhaps you'd better drive me back to my flat. I'll manage somehow.'

Cyn looked across at him in dismay; even in profile his face looked starkly unrelenting. God, what choice did she have—had she ever had? 'Of course you must come home with me,' she told him briskly, turning in her seat to restart the van. 'After all, it was my fault the accident happened at all, so I'm responsible for you until you're mobile again,' she accepted heavily, turning her attention to driving back to the cottage now; anything but dwelling on just how difficult it was going to be for her having Wolf invade the privacy of her home in this way.

'How graciously put,' Wolf drawled derisively.

Cyn gave him a sharp glance, hurriedly looking away again at the mocking humour in the wry twist of his mouth. Damn him, he had to know how much she dreaded the thought of being in such close proximity with him for the next—how long had the nurse said he had to rest? A couple of days, wasn't it? Cyn had never realised how long a couple of days could seem until that moment! And it was the weekend too, with no wedding to be involved in the organisation of, so there would be no respite for her by being able to go off to work either. God . . . !

She wasn't sure at that moment whether she was cursing—or praying!

'I'll need some things from my flat,' Wolf told her with a frown. 'Clothes, things like that. And my briefcase, of course,' he sighed heavily.

They had managed to get him into the cottage at last, and it hadn't been without a struggle. Everything had gone fine when they were outside, Wolf already seeming to have mastered the crutches quite competently. It had only been once they got inside the cottage that the problems presented themselves; there was too much furniture for him to be able to manoeuvre himself properly, and the low ceilings didn't help either. The only way he could get himself into the sitting-room at all was by Cyn actually moving half the furniture back against the walls, and so clearing a space for him in the middle of the room. All of which made it look very barren.

But Cyn had finally got him settled in an armchair beside the unlit fireplace, his foot resting up on a stool, the crutches conveniently placed in the nook beside the fireplace so that he could reach them easily. Having him here was going to be more than just disruptive to her peace of mind!

And now he was suggesting she go to his flat and collect some things for him! 'Do you still live in the same place?' She hoped not! The thought of going back there——

'Of course,' he replied smoothly, watching her with narrowed eyes as she visibly stiffened. 'Is there some problem with that?' he asked softly.

Not for him, obviously. But for her...! She and Wolf had first made love in that flat, had spent all their good times together there, making love, cooking together, laughing together, Wolf painting while she——

'No,' she told him thoughtfully. 'No, there's no problem with that at all.' She would finally be able to know what had happened to his paintings, whether he still had his studio there or if he had given all that up with all the other things that now seemed to be missing from his life. Things like laughter... And fun... Things like Wolf himself...! 'I'll go now, shall I?' She stood up ready to leave.

'That anxious to escape my company for a few hours, are you?' he rasped harshly. 'Oh, for God's sake...! Just take my keys and go.' He took the keys out of his pocket and thrust them at her before resting his head back against the chair once she had taken them, closing his eyes wearily.

Cyn continued to look down at him for several long minutes, her fingers closing about the cold keys, not knowing whether she should go or stay. He looked tired, very tired, but she didn't know whether that was from the pain of his ankle or something else; after all, no matter how disparaging she might have been about his reaction to Rebecca calling off the wedding, his fiancée *had* walked out on him today too.

'Wolf——'

'If you're going, just go!' His eyes were open now and he glared up at her. 'I don't need you to baby-sit me every minute of the day!'

Baby-sitting was the last thing she had in mind, but it was only just beginning to dawn on her exactly how incapacitated he was. For one thing, her downstairs loo was through the kitchen and out of the back door... It should be no problem with her here to help him, but on his own——!

'Er—Wolf...?' She chewed awkwardly on her bottom lip.

His impatience deepened. 'Just give me the newspaper, a pen so I can do the crossword, a glass of fruit juice or something so that I don't dehydrate while you make this mammoth trek into town.' His mouth twisted with his sarcasm. 'And——'

'The fruit juice might not be a good idea—not when the toilet is actually outside,' she explained with a grimace.

He drew in an irritated breath. 'OK, don't give me the newspaper *or* a pen to do the crossword, *or* the damned fruit juice; I'll just sit in the chair here and go to sleep till you get back! Will that do?' he challenged harshly, his hands clenched at his sides.

'I was only——'

'I know what you "were only", Cyn,' he sighed impatiently. 'I'm just not in any frame of mind to want to be bothered with it at the moment. Understand?' He looked up at her grimly.

Yes, she understood only too well. She was as quickly coming to learn the moods of this new Wolf as she had thought she knew the old one; he just wanted to be left alone, didn't want anything, especially not her fussing around him.

Nevertheless, she did pause in the kitchen long enough to get him a sandwich and some fruit; he hadn't had anything to eat for some time either. She placed them on the table next to him—with the requested fruit juice. Knowing Wolf, he would manage somehow, if he was desperate enough.

He had fallen asleep, she discovered when she turned to tell him about the food, his face completely relaxed now, the lines of pain and tiredness completely erased. He looked younger now, more like the Wolf she had once known—— No! This *wasn't* the Wolf she had known, or even thought she had known. This man was a hardened businessman, cut-throat, if the success of Thornton Industries was any indication. Besides, this Wolf had just had a second fiancée walk out on him, and for very similar reasons, if Barbara's appearance in his office yesterday was anything to go by. Why didn't he just marry the other woman and stop involving other people in their emotionally painful triangle?

For years after she had given Wolf his ring back Cyn had looked in the newspapers for just such an announcement. She had realised the two wouldn't be able to marry immediately, not when Barbara had only recently been widowed by Wolf's brother's death. But surely after a socially acceptable interval the two of them could have married? It didn't make sense to Cyn that they hadn't. But then nothing about Wolf's feelings for Barbara had ever made sense to her!

Cyn turned away abruptly without waking him, leaving the food and drink beside him; when he woke up he would see them there if he wanted them. She just needed to get out for a while, away from all those painful memories of her disillusionment with Wolf.

Not that going to his flat was going to do that, she accepted, feeling herself becoming more and more tense as she parked outside the building and crossed the pavement to press the security button. She and Wolf had forgotten all about that; she might have driven all this way to be literally turned away at the door. The flats in this prestigious block were such that a security guard screened everyone entering or leaving.

It was the same security man from seven years ago!

Cyn could hardly believe it, but she instantly recognised the slightly balding man as George Crossley from the time she had been such a regular visitor to Wolf's apartment that she had even had her own key. He was older now, of course—weren't they all!—and was slightly plumper than she remembered, slightly balder too, but it was definitely George.

'Miss Smith!' he greeted her with genuine pleasure as he unlocked the door to her, smiling broadly. 'It is Miss Smith, isn't it?' He seemed less certain now that he had had time to remember the fact that he hadn't seen her for several years.

'It certainly is, George,' she returned warmly, stepping inside. Just because he had recognised her it didn't mean he was going to calmly accept her going up to Wolf's penthouse flat, but if she was actually inside the building he might feel less inclined to throw her out again. 'Mr

Thornton has had a slight accident, I'm afraid, and——'

'Mr Thornton has?' He instantly looked concerned. 'Nothing serious, I hope?'

'Not in the least,' she assured him easily. 'But he's going to be staying with me for a few days, so I need to pick up some of his things from his flat. Is that all right?'

'But of course, Miss Smith,' he nodded without hesitation. 'I was always under strict instructions from Mr Thornton that if you should ever want to see him you were to do so straight away.'

That instruction was seven years old, and way out of date, but had obviously never been rescinded by Wolf. And if George was willing to accept that it still stood, who was she to quibble? As long as she got Wolf's things she didn't particularly care that George must wonder at her reappearance after a seven-year absence.

She didn't linger in the reception area. She didn't want to give the elderly man any time to perhaps wonder if he should be quite this welcoming to her after such a long time, so she gave him a friendly wave before stepping into the lift and pressing the button for the top floor.

The butterfly feeling in her stomach seemed to increase with each floor that was passed, and as the lift came to a smooth halt on the top floor Cyn thought she was actually going to be sick! She had never thought she would ever come back here again, to the place of her greatest happiness—and her greatest humiliation!

The décor was different, thank God, the carpets and furniture too, although the new colours of green and cream in the sitting-room were no more Wolf than the previous ones had been. But they would be a perfect foil

for a woman with flashing green eyes! came Cyn's unbidden thought.

Barbara had once again decorated this room for Wolf,
Cyn knew it as surely as if she had been told. The deep
green carpet, the pale cream suite, the subtle pale green
wallpaper, the ebony furniture; it was all Barbara, with
her black hair and dark green eyes.

This time the colour scheme had been continued into
the main bedroom, the king-size bed that had once
dominated the room now replaced with a huge four-
poster; even the tapestry drapes on this were mainly a
deep rich green.

Cyn took one glance around the room and hurried
through to the studio, seeking sanctuary. And finding
it!

It was the same! Exactly the same, she realised as her
pulse-rate steadied and her nerves calmed after her earlier
feelings of near-panic. Nothing had been moved at all.
Nothing...

Finished paintings still stood against the walls exactly
as she remembered them, half-finished canvases against
another wall, the painting Wolf had been working on
the last time Cyn was here still half completed on the
easel, as it had been the last time she saw it. Wolf hadn't
worked on his painting at all in the last seven years!

It was wicked. Sacrilege. Heartbreaking!

Cyn turned to leave the room as the tears threatened
to blind her, then was arrested in mid-flight as she saw
the painting of herself, the siren on the rocks.

The wall behind the door was bare of all other
paintings except the one of her, and a special light had
been fixed above it as the best way of lighting it. And
as Cyn flicked on the switch for this she saw exactly how
effective it was—the swirling sea seeming to take on new

life, reaching out, tempting, but having no impression on the hauntingly lovely woman who gazed serenely out over the rugged beauty, knowing she was impervious to its and any other danger.

Wolf had kept the painting which *she* had inspired... Even more significant, he had been in this room at least once in the last seven years, to supervise the hanging of this picture; he might even have hung it himself.

Why? came her next question. Admittedly it was Wolf's best work, but it was of *her*, unmistakably, irrefutably. It had been painted during those first days of their desire for each other. And it showed, in each brush-stroke.

Cyn couldn't stand looking at it any longer. She turned off the light to go back into the bedroom, opening and shutting the cupboards and drawers in there as she hurriedly took out the clothes she thought Wolf would need for the next few days, determinedly putting from her mind the intimacy of the fact that she knew exactly where to find those clothes. And the suitcase to put them in.

And yet she hesitated about leaving once the suitcase was packed. Obviously Wolf no longer painted, and for reasons she couldn't even guess at, but if it was merely because of a lack of time now that he had taken on the controls of Thornton Industries, he was going to be at the cottage with very little else to do for the next few days, despite his request for his briefcase; he wasn't going to get very far without the use of a telephone!

Without hesitating to give herself further time for thought Cyn went back into the studio and picked up the box of equipment Wolf had always taken with him if they went away for a couple of days, knowing it contained sketch-pads, pencils, charcoal, paints and brushes. She collected up one of the bare canvases too before leaving the room again, tucking that under her arm so that she could pick up the packed suitcase and the briefcase in one hand. If Wolf didn't want to paint, fine, but at least he would be given the opportunity to do so if he wished.

She was grateful for George's offer of help when she staggered out of the lift with all the luggage. She should really have brought the things down in two goes, but she just hadn't wanted to go back up to that flat for a second time; it reminded her too much of Barbara, and the place the other woman had always had in Wolf's life.

'A few days, hmm, Miss Smith?' George gave her a knowing wink before raising his hand in a farewell salute as she manoeuvred the van out into the traffic.

Any longer than that, Cyn vowed, her emotions raw from being in Wolf's flat, and she would personally drive him to his mother's and deposit him on the doorstep!

'What's that?'

Cyn looked up from carrying Wolf's things in to find him watching her across the short distance of the sitting-room. Amazingly he had still been asleep when she arrived back at the cottage a short time ago, and she could only presume the painkilling injection the nurse had given him at the hospital must be the reason for that; it wasn't like Wolf to take naps in the day. At least, not the Wolf she knew. And she was sure the head of Thornton Industries didn't usually have the time to take naps—in the day, or any other time either!

She had tried to be as quiet as possible, removing the stale sandwich to the kitchen before starting to bring in the luggage. But she obviously hadn't been quiet enough. Wolf was looking at her with narrowed eyes now as she put the things down on the carpeted floor.

'I said what's that?' His voice was icily sharp now as he sat forward in the chair.

Cyn gave him an exasperated look. 'Your things, of course,' she said impatiently. 'That *is* where I've been the last couple of hours.'

Wolf nodded abruptly. 'To get me a change of clothes, and my briefcase, yes,' he accepted harshly. 'But that isn't either of those things.' He gave a sharp inclination of his head in the direction of the canvas she had propped up against the front of the dresser.

It had been a long day, she was tired, she didn't need for him to state the obvious. 'I think I'm well aware of that,' she said wearily, desperate for her dinner now; the apple she had taken with her to munch along the way just hadn't been enough. 'Would you like——?'

'I'd like an answer to my question,' he rasped coldly, every muscle and sinew in his body tense now.

'And *I* would like my dinner,' Cyn told him sharply. 'I've been running all over town for you for one reason or another this evening, and now I would like to eat.' Her eyes flashed deeply violet. 'Just because you've woken up feeling like a bear with a sore head, don't think you can use me as your verbal punch-bag; I'm hungry, I'm tired, and I'm just not in the mood!' The last came out emotionally; today hadn't been easy for her either, damn it.

Wolf moved forward in his seat, carefully avoiding putting any weight on his bandaged injured ankle. 'I said you could go to my flat and collect some clothes for me, I didn't say you could go poking about in rooms that you have no right to be in!' he bit out harshly, his eyes glittering deeply golden, his mouth a thin, taut line. 'No one goes in my studio. No one!'

Cyn glared back across the room at him, her hands aggressively on her hips; she had really meant it when she said she was too tired and hungry for this, in fact she was at the end of her endurance. And what did he mean, he had *said* she could go to his flat and pick up some things for him? He had *ordered* her to do so!

'Not even you, apparently!' she challenged scornfully.

Wolf became very still, only a nerve pulsing in his cheek now to show he wasn't completely carved out of granite. 'Not even me,' he echoed softly, dangerously so. 'So whatever you've brought with you from in there, you can damn well take it back again.'

She gave a weary sigh. 'Wolf——'

'I mean it, Cyn,' he grated tautly, his whole body tense with suppressed anger—and it was only suppressed because he was in no position, immobile as he was, to do anything about it! 'I don't want those things here. I don't want them anywhere near me!'

Cyn could see that he meant it, knew by the implacability of his expression that he wanted the canvas, and the box containing his painting things, removed, that he would be happier never having to see them again.

It was almost as if he hated the things that had once given him his purpose in life...

CHAPTER SEVEN

CYN looked at him frowningly. 'Don't you think you're behaving a little childishly now——?'

'I don't give a damn what I'm behaving!' Wolf struggled to his feet, supporting himself with the crutches as he did so. 'You had no right bringing those things here——'

'Oh, no—I only have the *right* to run around after you like some obedient slave!' she acknowledged scornfully.

He drew in a harsh breath. 'You don't have to do that either,' he ground out angrily. 'I've changed my mind about staying here, Cyn; I think I'd like to go back to my flat after all.'

Cyn stared at him incredulously. *He* was the one who had made her feel so guilty about his accident that she'd had no choice but to invite him to stay here until he felt better. He was also the one who had insisted he needed his things from his flat. A trip into town she had just spent the last two hours on, forgoing her dinner into the bargain to do it. And now he said he had changed his mind and wanted to leave after all—well, he could just think again!

She glared at him now, her mouth firm. 'I don't give a damn what you think, Wolf,' she told him forcefully. 'You were the one who wanted to stay here, and now you can damn well do so!'

He looked taken aback at her aggression, and Cyn couldn't help wondering how long it was since anyone had stood up to him in this way; as head of Thornton Industries he no doubt didn't meet too much opposition to his proposals. Well, he was on her territory now, not Thornton Industries', nor his family's, and if he thought she was going to run around pandering to his whims he was mistaken; besides, his original reason for wanting to stay here still stood—he could not go back to his flat to cope on his own until he became more adept with the crutches, and as he said going back to his mother's house was out of the question too...

Finally he relaxed slightly, his mouth twisting in mocking humour. 'You can't make me stay here, Cyn,' he derided.

'No?' She arched her brows. 'And just how do you propose leaving? Are you going to call for a taxi to take you? Sorry, Wolf, but, as you should know, the telephone is out of order. Or are you going to hobble away on your crutches?' she taunted as his humour faded again and he began to frown darkly; obviously he had forgotten the telephone was out of order! 'Excuse me for saying so, Wolf, but I don't think you'd get very far!'

His eyes were narrowed. 'Let me get this straight, Cyn,' he said softly. 'Are you telling me I'm a prisoner here?'

'Hardly!' Her brows rose again. 'What I am telling you is that if you can get someone to transport you away from here, fine, go ahead and do it, but *I'm* not driving you anywhere!' And as if to prove her point she walked off to the kitchen to begin preparing dinner. For both of them. She didn't think Wolf would be going anywhere—not tonight, at least.

She sensed his presence in the kitchen doorway minutes later as much as heard him; he really was having trouble with those crutches, she thought with amusement. 'Spaghetti bolognese, all right?' she enquired lightly, already chopping the onions and mushrooms in preparation.

His expression was harshly distant, his mouth a bitter twist. 'You know, I once used to fantasise about the two of us being alone together in a remote cottage somewhere, with no phones or family for distraction.' He shook his head self-derisively. 'What a fool I was!'

Cyn frowned. 'Wolf——'

'No dinner for me, thank you,' he told her abruptly. 'I think I'll go to bed.'

She put down the knife she had been using to chop the onions, turning fully to face him in the small confines of the kitchen. 'But you've only just woken up,' she pointed out reasonably. 'And you must be hungry.'

He gave a rueful grimace and turned away. 'Not for food,' he muttered as he limped off.

Cyn moved over to the doorway. 'What did you say?' She halted him at the bottom of the narrow staircase, frowning deeply.

'I said I was a fool,' he told her grimly. 'You're right, Cyn, the past is the past—and it should remain there!'

She didn't know if he was still talking about his painting now, or if it was something else, but she knew now wasn't the time to ask him which it was; the harshness of his expression was enough to warn her against doing so.

Just as it was enough to deter her from offering to help him manoeuvre the stairs too! There were only a dozen or so steps altogether, but it was a narrow staircase, making it impossible for him to use both crutches to support himself with, a fact he soon realised, as he threw one of the crutches impatiently down on to the sitting-room floor, leaning heavily on the handrail to lever himself up the steps.

He was a big man, lean but muscled, and probably weighed a hundred and eighty pounds, and the handrail was only supported by a few screws, but Cyn thought he could be in danger of throwing his other crutch at her if she should point this out—so she wisely kept silent, going back into the kitchen to prepare her own dinner and leaving him to it.

But she could hear him, and knew just how difficult it was for him to get up the stairs. She longed to go and help him, but was sure her help would be rejected. And she had suffered enough rejections from Wolf to last her a lifetime!

Her breath left her in a sigh of relief as she at last heard him reach the top of the stairs, surprising her, because she hadn't realised she had been holding her breath until that moment. God, this Wolf was so complex and difficult. Why had he been so upset about the canvas and paints? It wasn't so important, surely, that he had to become so angry about it? Of course she was curious, deeply curious, she admitted, to know why he no longer painted, but his reaction to just seeing those things had been totally unexpected.

There were so many things about this Wolf that she didn't understand, so many things she would have liked to ask him—but knew she never would——

'Damn!' she muttered distractedly as she saw she was burning the onions and mushrooms, and lifted the frying-pan off the top of the cooker to let it cool down a little.

She couldn't allow herself to brood over Wolf; she had done enough of that in the past. She should have let him go earlier when he wanted to leave, should have been grateful to drive him wherever he wanted to go, instead of condemning herself to spending yet more time in his company. And if he hadn't made her so angry she would have done, she sighed. The thing was, how did she stop herself from becoming angry at his behaviour?

She was doing it again, allowing herself to be completely caught up in thoughts of Wolf instead of getting on with her life! Dinner. *She* was going to eat even if Wolf wasn't; she well deserved her dinner after the day she had had!

She wished she could actually say she enjoyed her spaghetti, but the truth of the matter was that, aware of Wolf up the stairs as she was, her appetite was completely ruined. His luggage still sitting at the bottom of the stairs, along with that discarded crutch, didn't help matters either, and she took his case and the other things upstairs as soon as she had finished her meal; maybe if she didn't have to look at them she could forget he was even in the cottage! It was doubtful, but worth a try.

Her eyes widened in dismay when she quietly opened the door to the small guest bedroom and saw Wolf sprawled asleep on top of the bare mattress; she had completely forgotten that the spare bed wasn't made up. And obviously Wolf had been in no mood to tell her it wasn't. Or perhaps he had thought, given her own rebellious mood, that she might refuse to make it up for him. She wouldn't, of course, but he probably hadn't thought it was worth the hassle. Or else, and this was more likely, he just hadn't wanted to see her again tonight.

Oh, this was ridiculous, she decided as she gazed down at him as he slept. They were both behaving like children, rather than the twenty-seven and thirty-five they really were!

Not that Wolf looked thirty-five now that he was relaxed in sleep, the lines of cynicism smoothed from his face now, his mouth no longer that grim line but as lovingly sensual as Cyn remembered it.

She sat down abruptly in the small bedroom chair facing him, putting down the case and canvas she had been carrying. Where had it all gone wrong for them? *Why* had it all gone wrong? The answer to both those questions was supplied in just a single word—Barbara...

Cyn had known Claudia Thornton didn't approve of her as Wolf's choice of bride, but she had seemed to accept that she didn't have too much say in the matter, that Wolf had made his mind up, so she might as well accept the *fait accompli* with good grace if she couldn't exactly feel happy about it. What *Cyn* hadn't known was that at the time Claudia would have been willing to accept any bride Wolf chose as long as a family scandal was avoided; it would have ripped the Thornton family apart, thrown them all into the public limelight, if Barbara Thornton had divorced one brother to go to the other one!

Cyn could still remember her humiliation at realising she had just been second-best to Wolf, a smoke-screen to the affair he was having with his brother's wife. But there had been no need for pretence once Alex Thornton was killed in that air crash.

Wolf had hurriedly telephoned Cyn while she was on duty in Reception at the hotel to tell her the news, obviously in shock, but knowing it was his responsibility to sort out all the details necessary after such a tragedy. Cyn had been stunned herself at the death, even though she didn't know Wolf's brother very well. Alex Thornton hadn't liked her any more than his mother did, but he had always been extremely polite—something, she had learnt the evening she first met Wolf, that showed Alex's displeasure!—on the few occasions they had met. It certainly didn't seem fair that such a young man, a man with an astute brain and endless vitality, should have been killed in such a way. And because he was Wolf's brother, Cyn had necessarily been involved in the tragedy.

Not that the two brothers had been especially close, they were too different in personality for that. Wolf was relaxed and charming, Alex a hard-headed businessman. But that didn't change the fact that Alex had been Wolf's brother, and that a bond of affection had existed between them, albeit usually from a distance.

'I'll get off work now and come over, shall I?' Cyn offered as soon as Wolf told her the news.

'There's no point,' he instantly refused. 'I'm going to be pretty tied up with Mother and Barbara at the house for a while.'

She appreciated that, but surely as his fiancée she should at least be at his side during this ordeal? Having no family of her own, she appreciated that she could only guess at how devastated the two Thornton women must be by their loss, but surely there must be something *she* could do to help?

'How are your mother and Barbara?' she asked sympathetically.

'How the hell do you think——?' Wolf broke off immediately, sighing deeply. 'They're both in a hell of a state,' he told her grimly. 'Mother's collapsed, Barbara's hysterical—it's just a bloody mess.'

Cyn didn't need to be told of the strain he was under; she could hear it in his voice. 'I should be there, Wolf——'

'No!' he rasped harshly.

She flinched at his obvious anger at the suggestion. 'But I'm sure I could——'

'I said there's no point, Cyn,' Wolf snapped irritably. 'Look, I have to go,' he told her curtly. 'I'll talk to you later.' He rang off abruptly.

Cyn became aware of the other receptionist eyeing her curiously as she sat cradling the telephone receiver long after the line had been disconnected, slowly putting the receiver down as she saw that curiosity, her thoughts still on Wolf. He was upset, of course he was; he couldn't have realised how hurtful he was being by seeming to shut her out in this way. The last thing he needed now was for her to over-react to his distraction; he had his mother's and Barbara's feelings to cope with just now, that was enough!

But it wasn't easy finishing her early evening shift, trying to act as if everything were normal. The hotel staff would be informed of Alex's death as soon as it became public knowledge, Cyn was sure, but in the meantime she didn't think Wolf would want her to talk about it. All the people she worked with were aware of her engagement to Wolf Thornton, and for the most part they had been nice about it, with only the occasional bitchy comment about her 'marrying the boss', and a curiosity as to why she was continuing to work at all when that was so. The latter was easy to answer as far as Cyn herself was concerned; as she had grown up in an orphanage and foster-homes, where money had always been in short supply, it would be completely against her nature not to work to support herself, a fact Wolf respected, although he had warned her he might not feel the same way after they were married. It was something they could argue out at the time, she had told him.

Nevertheless, she was more than a little relieved that evening when her shift came to an end, picking up some groceries from the convenience store nearest Wolf's flat on the way there; if things had been as horrendous for him this evening as she imagined they had, food would have been the last thing on his mind. And although he might not feel like eating, he would feel better for it if he did.

She let herself in with her key as usual, knowing Wolf wasn't home when she walked into the silence of the flat. Of course, she realised disappointedly, if his mother had broken down, he was probably still at the house. Never mind, he would be home some time this evening, and when he was she would have a meal and some sympathy ready for him; she doubted if either woman had given his feelings a second thought in their own grief.

She stayed at Wolf's flat more than at her own now, keeping a lot of her clothes here, and was going into the bedroom to change out of the uniform suit and blouse she wore to work. But before she could open the bedroom door it was opened from the other side. Wolf, she realised happily. He was here after all.

'Darling, is that you?' asked the unmistakable voice of Barbara Thornton.

As the bedroom door opened wider Cyn could see the other woman as well as hear her, and as she took in the sheer pale green nightgown and matching négligé Barbara was wearing she took a step back, her cheeks paling. What was Barbara doing here, in Wolf's bedroom? And why was she dressed like that?

Green eyes narrowed as Barbara looked at Cyn. 'I thought you were Wolf,' she said coldly.

'Darling' was Wolf? What on earth——?

'Don't look so stunned, Lucynda,' Barbara drawled derisively, walking out of the bedroom into the sitting-room, her silk nightclothes moving lovingly against the voluptuous curves of her body. 'I've been calling Wolf "darling" for longer than I can remember,' she dismissed in a bored voice.

Not in front of Cyn she hadn't, nor other members of the family, as far as Cyn knew. She watched the other woman as she strolled across the room to open the gold cigarette box that stood on the coffee-table—a cigarette box Cyn had never been able to understand being here at all, and always filled, when Wolf didn't smoke. Could it possibly be for Barbara's benefit, and, if so, why?

Cyn still didn't move, couldn't, as the other woman took out a cigarette before lighting it, drawing on it deeply before turning back to look at Cyn with mockingly raised brows. This was the woman who was supposed to be hysterical? Anyone less hysterical Cyn had yet to see. Barbara looked completely in control of herself—and the situation!

Barbara watched her through a cloud of smoke, her mouth twisted mockingly. 'Penny dropped yet, has it?' she finally drawled.

Thoughts were crowding in on Cyn that she didn't want to know, incredible, unbelievable thoughts that just couldn't be true. And yet...

'I'm sorry about Alex,' Cyn said abruptly, still staring at the other woman with disbelieving fascination. What she was thinking just couldn't be true. It couldn't!

Barbara stiffened at the mention of her husband, green eyes narrowing to hardened slits. 'So am I,' she acknowledged harshly. 'Death is so—final. It isn't the way I ever wanted things to turn out.'

Cyn frowned again; what did the other woman mean by that? 'Where's Wolf?' she prompted shortly.

Some of the tension left Barbara now, and she drew on her cigarette once again. 'With his mother,' she dismissed. 'He's joining me here when he can get away.'

Cyn swallowed hard. 'You're expecting him back tonight, then?' She so desperately needed to talk to him, to be reassured that the things she was imagining weren't true. And only Wolf could do that...

'Oh, yes,' Barbara's voice softened, 'he promised me he wouldn't leave me alone for long. He knows how much I need him tonight.'

And the other woman had been waiting for him in his bedroom. Wolf! Cyn cried inwardly. I need you, I need you to tell me this is all a horrendous mistake, that Barbara doesn't mean what I think she means!

But those thoughts kept crowding in on her—Wolf's abruptness with her on the telephone earlier, his telling her not to go to his mother's house, that there was no point in her being there. Surely there would have been every point if she could be there for him? Unless... He didn't need her there for him, not now that Barbara was free...?

It couldn't be true, it couldn't. Wolf loved her, had asked her to marry him. And yet those doubts niggled away at her now, refused to go away.

Barbara still watched her with narrowed eyes, sitting down in one of the armchairs, crossing one silky leg over the other. 'I'll tell him you called, shall I?' she drawled derisively at Cyn's confused expression.

'I——' Cyn moistened lips suddenly gone dry. 'I'll wait for him,' she decided, although the thought of sitting here with this woman while she did so was completely unappealing to her; there was certainly nothing for the two of them to talk about, it was Wolf Cyn wanted to talk to, not Barbara!

The other woman gave her a pitying look. 'Do you think that's wise?'

Cyn swallowed hard. 'Wise?' she echoed shakily, reaction definitely beginning to set in.

Barbara gave an impatient sigh. 'Oh, grow up, Lucynda, do!' she instructed irritably as she viciously stubbed out the cigarette. 'You really can't be this naïve! Surely it's obvious to you by now that Wolf and I have been having an affair for years, that——'

'No!' Cyn put her hands up over her ears as the other woman said the things she had tried not to even put into thoughts. 'Wolf loves me. He—— We're engaged!' She held up her left hand triumphantly, her ring sparkling brightly as she did so.

'Hmm, a stroke of genius on Wolf's part, that,' Barbara nodded ruefully. 'Alex was becoming suspicious about the two of us, you see,' she explained lightly. 'And then by a stroke of luck Wolf met you the night of his mother's birthday party. Of course, it originally started out with Wolf just wanting to paint you, but during the course of the evening we both realised that Alex's dark mood that night was due to suspicions about the two of us rather than Wolf's lateness, so Wolf decided a bit of camouflage was in order——'

'Wolf did?' Cyn choked in dismay.

'Oh, he would have made love to you anyway, Lucynda,' Barbara told her dismissively. 'He always did like to make love to his models. But I knew it didn't mean anything, that I was the only constant in his life. Ask him to show you the painting he did of me some time,' she added huskily. 'I'm sure you'll find it very enlightening.'

Just the tone of her voice told Cyn exactly what sort of painting it would be! It was no good saying she didn't believe the other woman, because she did. It all made so much sense now—the fevered way Wolf had painted

her that first night, the way he had been late for their
date, the announcement that very first evening that he
intended marrying her. It had all been as a cover-up for
his affair with his brother's wife. And now Barbara was
free...

Cyn straightened in jerky movements. 'I'd better go,'
she said abruptly, needing to get away now, before she
broke down. She pulled off her engagement ring.
'Perhaps you could give this to Wolf,' she held the ring
out to the other woman. 'I won't be needing it any more.'

Barbara made no effort to take the ring from her.
'Don't be such a coward, Lucynda,' she taunted softly.
'You at least owe Wolf the courtesy of giving him his
ring back in person.'

Cyn wanted to hurl it into his face, to tell him just
what she thought of him and the way he had used her,
but she knew if she did that she would break down completely, and these two had already hurt and humiliated
her enough. She had loved Wolf so much, and he had
just been using her!

She put the ring down on the coffee-table. 'I—— Tell
him I've changed my mind, that—that I realise I don't
want to marry him after all.' She spoke quickly, knowing
that what she really wanted to do was beg and plead
with Wolf, to tell him he was making a mistake, that *she*
was the one who could make him happy—while at the
same time she knew there was no future for them now,
that it was over, the whole impossible dream. 'Tell him
I've realised it's Roger I love!' she claimed in defence,
running to the door before the tears could fall and totally
humiliate her.

'Roger?' Barbara echoed with a frown. 'I won't even
pretend to know who he is,' she dismissed scathingly.
'But I can assure you, knowing Wolf as I do, that he

isn't the sort of man who'll want his ring back now that your—relationship is over. And believe me,' she added hardly, 'it is over!'

'Wolf, apparently, is only the sort of man who has an affair with his brother's wife while using another woman as a shield to that affair!' Cyn shot back insultingly, two bright spots of colour in her cheeks now.

Barbara shrugged. 'You've had your uses, I must admit.'

'Not any more,' Cyn said tautly. 'Find someone else to cover up your sordid little affair until you no longer need to do so; I don't intend doing it any longer!'

She fled out into the night, desperate to escape, going to the person she knew would take her in without asking questions: Roger.

She had met Roger at the last foster-home she had lived in when she was sixteen. He was the eldest son of the house, away at university most of the time, but becoming one of her best friends during the times he was home on holiday. Once she'd left the Collins household and moved into rooms of her own the two of them had remained on friendly terms, and had gone out together on a very casual basis after that. Roger had been full of foreboding when she fell so instantly in love with Wolf, but he had been happy for her when the two of them became engaged. Although Cyn didn't think he would be exactly surprised at the way things had turned out; Roger had never been a hundred per cent certain of her relationship with Wolf, despite the engagement. How right he had been to feel wary!

Roger took one look at her, as she stood so woefully on his doorstep, before taking her inside, giving her a warming glass of brandy, then tucking her up beneath the bedcovers in his spare bedroom—all without asking her a single question. And Cyn knew why when she caught a glimpse of herself in the bathroom mirror; she was pale as a ghost, with a haunted look in her eyes that showed her innermost pain and disillusionment. That told its own story.

Roger urged her to stay on at his flat with him the next day, but Cyn declined his offer, knowing she had to face this, intending to go to work at lunchtime for her shift at the hotel as usual. She had never run away from a situation in her life; she had had to be tough, with the childhood she had known, and she wouldn't leave her job at Thornton's Hotel until she had found another one. And if her presence there embarrassed the Thornton family, all well and good; that was nothing to the suffering she had known during the long sleepless night that had just passed, and all the other long sleepless nights yet to come.

She hadn't been at work for longer than ten minutes when she saw Wolf enter the hotel, and her face paled as he walked across with long forceful strides to where she stood on duty at the reception desk. Not here, she cried inwardly. Oh, God, not here!

If she felt ill, he looked grim, seeming to have aged overnight, with lines beside his eyes and mouth that she was sure hadn't been there the last time she saw him. Was that only just over twenty-four hours ago? It seemed a lifetime!

Of course, Alex's death was bound to have had an effect on him—even if it was only guilt at having an affair with his brother's wife while he had been alive!

Cyn straightened defensively as he reached the desk, ignoring the curious stares of the other receptionists as she met Wolf's gaze unflinchingly. If he wanted this to be a public scene, then so be it!

'Where were you all night?' he demanded without greeting, his eyes steely gold slits.

Where had she been all night? Why, *she* was the one who should have been accusingly asking that of him, *and* who he had been with! 'I went to the flat, Wolf,' she told him evenly. 'I—— Didn't Barbara tell you?' Or had the two been so engrossed in each other on Wolf's return the previous night that the other woman hadn't got around to telling him that?

'Yes, she told me,' he rasped. 'And when she gave me this,' he held her engagement ring in the palm of one hand now, the diamonds blinking dazzlingly, 'I telephoned your flat to find out what was going on, but there was no reply. Or this morning either, for that matter,' he ground out harshly. 'Where the hell were you, Cyn?' he demanded again.

Perhaps this wasn't the place for this conversation, Cyn decided again as she could see the other receptionists openly watching the exchange now, the engagement ring in Wolf's hand indicating the seriousness of the conversation. All the hotel staff had been agog with the news of Alex Thornton's death when she arrived for work earlier. They would have a field-day with the fact that Cyn's engagement to Wolf Thornton now appeared to be in trouble.

Cyn moved out from behind the desk. 'Let's go somewhere a little more private to discuss this,' she suggested tightly, not waiting for Wolf's reply but leading the way over to the small conference-room, across the reception area, that she knew wasn't in use today. She could feel Wolf's brooding presence behind her as she walked that distance, so she didn't need to turn and look at him to know he was following her! She turned to him once she had closed the door quietly behind them, instantly shutting out the sounds of the hotel and enclosing them in an expectant silence.

'Well?' Wolf prompted impatiently, hands thrust into his trouser pockets now.

Cyn looked at his appearance properly, noting the unaccustomed dark suit and sober shirt and tie; obviously he had people to see today concerning his brother's funeral arrangements. 'This is a painful time for both of us, Wolf,' she gave a weary sigh. 'Let's just accept that we made a mistake and leave it at that.'

He glowered across the room at her. 'And if I don't want to?'

'I don't think you have any choice, Wolf,' Cyn shook her head sadly. 'It's all over between us now. Even if— things were different,' although she couldn't envisage that he and Barbara would give up their relationship now! 'I could never forget what you did to Alex.'

Wolf paled, seeming to sway slightly on his feet before regaining control of himself once again, breathing deeply. 'Do you think I don't feel guilty enough about that already, without——? My God, Cyn, I need you with me now, not for you to turn against me!' he told her raggedly, pain etched into his face.

What he meant was that he still needed her to act as a shield to his affair with Barbara; it would be even more scandalous if that relationship should become public knowledge so soon after Alex's death!

She shook her head again. 'I won't live that lie any longer, Wolf. I'm sorry about Alex's death, I really am,' she said with genuine regret. 'But at the same time it's made me realise what a mistake I was making even thinking the two of us could get married. Roger——'

'Were you with him last night?' Wolf realised incredulously.

She met his gaze unflinchingly. 'I spent the night at Roger's flat with him, yes,' she confirmed steadily; let Wolf leave her her dignity, at least, she pleaded inwardly. Couldn't he see what all this was doing to her?

'I thought Barbara had——' He broke off abruptly, frowning darkly. 'It's over, then,' he said heavily.

Cyn swallowed hard. 'Yes, it's over,' she told him huskily, willing herself not to cry. Not until Wolf had gone, anyway. Then she knew she wouldn't be able to stop the flood that threatened to drown her. 'It should never have begun really, should it?' she sighed.

'I wanted you from the very first moment I saw you,' he rasped.

As he wanted all the women he painted. Their relationship had only gone the one step further to an engagement because of the fear he and Barbara had that Alex would discover their affair. 'It isn't enough, Wolf,' Cyn said abruptly. 'Not for me. There has to be more to a relationship, a sharing, a—a trusting,' and she had trusted him implicitly until last night! 'Roger and I—— He knows me, understands me, he doesn't have—other commitments that will take him away from me. That's what I want from the man in my life.' She looked at Wolf unflinchingly, willing him to go now.

He continued to look at her searchingly for several long minutes, and then he let out a harsh breath as he could see she meant what she said. 'I hope you'll be happy, Cyn,' he said huskily.

She gave an inclination of her head. 'I hope you will be too.'

His mouth twisted bitterly. 'I don't think there's much chance of that,' he rasped before going to the door. But still he didn't leave, hesitating there before turning back to her. 'If you should change your mind——'

'I won't,' she assured him hurriedly; she might want to, but she knew that she wouldn't, that she had to be first and foremost in the life of the man she eventually— if ever!—married. And somehow she doubted now that she would...

Wolf nodded abruptly. 'I somehow thought you'd say that. But believe me, Cyn, no matter how much you might think you hate me, you can't be any more disgusted with me than I am with myself!' he told her before quietly leaving.

Cyn stared down at him now, sleeping so peacefully, and she couldn't help wondering once again what had happened to him during the last seven years.

He and Barbara had never married, although the other woman still seemed to be very much a factor in his life. Not that that was anything to go on. Roger was still a very important part of her life too. But her relationship with Roger had always been like that of brother and sister, had never contained any of the intimacy there had been between Wolf and Barbara, and it never would, either; Roger had someone very special in his life, and had done so for some time.

And Cyn couldn't even begin to guess at the part Rebecca Harcourt played in Wolf's life—or *had* played in it; the girl seemed to have decided she no longer wanted to be part of his life at all.

What Cyn did know, without a doubt, was that Wolf was in her bed again—albeit in her spare room—even though she had sworn it would never happen!

CHAPTER EIGHT

'COME on, Cyn, open up!' encouraged a slightly impatient voice.

Cyn stumbled down the stairs in answer to the knock on the front door, pushing the tumble of her hair back from her face and tying the belt to her robe as she hurried across the small sitting-room to open the front door, blinking as the bright April sunlight instantly dazzled her, focusing on Roger with difficulty as he stood on the doorstep.

'You weren't still in bed?' he complained. 'Have you forgotten we have a round of golf booked this morning?' He didn't wait for an answer to his first question; her state of undress was answer enough. He strode past her into the sitting-room, only five feet eight inches tall in his shoes, and so having no difficulty with the low height of the ceiling.

As Wolf did, Cyn remembered suddenly, glancing almost guiltily up the stairs. She hated to think what Roger would have to say on the subject if he should realise not only that she had met Wolf again, but that he was actually asleep upstairs! Roger had been so volubly disgusted with Wolf's behaviour seven years ago when Cyn had finally found the courage to tell him what had happened to her that night, and he was sure to be far from polite if he should ever meet Wolf again. She would just have to hope Wolf stayed asleep until after Roger had left.

And she had forgotten their customary round of golf on a Sunday morning, had forgotten today *was* Sunday! 'I——' she began.

'My fault, I'm afraid,' drawled a lightly mocking voice.

Cyn spun round sharply to see Wolf standing in the kitchen doorway, fully dressed, and drinking a cup of coffee, telling her that, despite her hopes, he had obviously been up for some time! And what did he mean, it was 'his fault'? She eyed him suspiciously—mainly because she dared not even look at Roger, sure he would have recognised the other man by now; Wolf really hadn't changed that much.

Wolf seemed completely relaxed and in control as he looked at the two of them across the room, one brow arched sardonically. 'I'm afraid after our rather—disturbed night,' Wolf continued dismissively, 'Cyn was in desperate need of a lie-in, so I just left her to it.' He shrugged.

Cyn almost gasped out loud at the obvious implication of Wolf's words; he had all but told Roger the two of them had spent the night together and Cyn had needed the lie-in because she was exhausted from it! Not only was it a blatant lie, it was also highly unlikely, when he was all but incapacitated by his twisted ankle. Although...perhaps not, she blushed as she recalled the past intimacy of their lovemaking.

She wished she could have controlled that blush the moment she felt her cheeks grow warm with it. Roger was looking at her with dismay as *he* saw that blush as coy embarrassment on her part!

'Coffee, anyone?' Wolf offered with feigned innocence.

Feigned—because he knew exactly what sort of impression he had just created! 'Not for me,' snapped Cyn, glaring at him before turning back to Roger. 'I met Wolf again quite by accident a couple of days ago——'

'I'm sure Roger isn't interested in all the details of how we met again,' Wolf cut in affectionately, walking across the room towards them, without the crutches and with a hardly noticeable limp, the bandage hidden by a black sock; the long rest from yesterday evening, and then a good night's sleep, seemed to have worked wonders with his injured ankle.

Unless it had never been as painfully incapacitating as it had seemed! Cyn eyed him suspiciously as he reached her side; surely he couldn't have been exaggerating his injury yesterday? And if so, why?

'It's enough that we did,' Wolf added huskily, standing closer to Cyn than she would have wished, his arm brushing against hers.

Increasing that impression of intimacy to Roger, Cyn realised frustratedly. 'If you give me five minutes to change, Roger,' she told him a little desperately, 'I'll join you for that round of golf.' Once she could talk to Roger alone she could explain to him what had really happened yesterday; with Wolf in this mischief-making mood, there was little point in trying to do it now!

Roger looked more confused than dismayed now—as well he might, Cyn thought resentfully, moving determinedly away from Wolf's side; they looked too much like a couple, standing side by side in that way.

'We can give it a miss this morning, if you'd prefer,' Roger said flatly, his expression grim as he looked at the other man.

The two men had met rarely in the past, but once again Cyn was struck by the physical differences in them. Wolf was at least six inches taller than the other man, and Roger looked boyish with his thick dark hair falling down over his forehead, his physique boyish too, with none of the muscular strength Wolf took so much for granted. Wolf had always possessed a maturity over the younger man, but that cynical hardness, which was so much a part of Wolf now, added to the impression, instantly putting Roger at a disadvantage.

'Sit down and I'll get you a cup of coffee while you're waiting,' Cyn suggested lightly to Roger; if the two men were sitting down their physical differences wouldn't be so noticeable! She gave a nervous start as Wolf reached out to grasp her arm as she walked past him towards the kitchen, looking up at him apprehensively now, his fingers a warm caress against her wrist.

'I'd like a refill too,' he told her huskily, holding out the empty mug he carried, his eyes as warm as molten gold as he smiled at her.

Cyn was totally disconcerted by his behaviour, taking the mug in jerky movements, carefully avoiding her hand making contact with his, moving away so that the hand on her wrist fell away ineffectually. She only just stopped herself heaving a sigh of relief at being released, instantly feeling angry with herself for being affected at all; Wolf was nothing to her now but an unnecessary nuisance, and the sooner he was out of her life again the better!

'I'll have the coffee,' Roger accepted distantly as he sat down, glancing at his wristwatch. 'But then I think I'll get back. I half promised my mother I'd call in for lunch.'

Cyn knew this was only an excuse to leave, that the two of them would normally have played golf for three or four hours before having a late lunch at the clubhouse, and then they would probably have visited Sheila together. Cyn had kept up her contact with all the Collins family, and had stayed with Sheila for several weeks after her husband died five years ago. She often just called in now to make sure her ex-foster-mother was all right.

'I'll get the coffee and then we can talk about it,' Cyn said firmly, and went off to the kitchen, being as quick as she could, unsure of what the two men would find to say to each other once they were left alone.

Wolf had no right to look so relaxed and happy this morning, she thought disgruntledly as she prepared the mugs of coffee. After she had left him in the spare bedroom last night, having covered him up with a duvet from the cupboard, she hadn't been able to fall asleep herself at all, but lay awake for a long time after she had climbed into bed, deeply disturbed by Wolf's presence in her home. He looked as if he had slept like a baby all night. His mood this morning bore no resemblance to the anger he had shown the previous evening when she returned with his painting equipment. It was like being in the same house with Dr Jekyll and Mr Hyde!

She had completely forgotten her habitual game of golf with Roger. Not that she could have done anything about putting him off even if she had remembered, not with the telephone out of action. Damn.

The two men weren't talking at all when she returned with the mugs of coffee. Not that Wolf looked particularly bothered by that fact, although Roger looked less than comfortable in the other man's company. Cyn sympathised with him; she often felt that way herself with Wolf now!

'Thanks.' Wolf took his coffee mug with another heart-stopping smile in her direction, sitting on the sofa now, perfectly relaxed and at ease. 'This is quite like old times, isn't it?' he said happily.

Cyn was going to hit him in a minute if he didn't stop playing games; he was as aware as they were that the three of them had never had 'old times', that he and Roger had only met three times, and on each occasion they had been like adversaries eyeing each other across a boxing-ring!

'Hardly.' Roger was the one to answer him drily. 'You may as well know, Thornton, that I'm no more happy about your involvement with Cyn this time around than I was the last time,' he told him grimly. 'And if you——'

'Roger, please!' she groaned in embarrassment, looking at him pleadingly.

'No, let him have his say,' Wolf said softly, his gaze fixed steadily on the other man.

Roger's mouth twisted. 'I intended to,' he assured them drily. 'If you hurt Cyn again I'll personally see to it that you suffer as much as she did last time.'

'Really?' There was a dangerous stillness about Wolf at the threat. 'And just how do you intend doing that?'

'I——'

'You may as well stop this now,' Cyn cut in firmly. 'Because there's no way Wolf is going to hurt me again,' she told Roger determinedly; Wolf couldn't hurt her once she had got him back to his flat and never had to see him again. And she intended doing that as soon as possible; he was obviously quite capable of taking care of himself today.

'Cyn's right.' Wolf spoke huskily. 'I have no intention of hurting her.'

'What you intend,' Roger told him, blue eyes narrowed, 'and what you actually do, seem to be two completely different things. Why couldn't you stay out of her life, Thornton?' he said harshly.

'I told you, Roger,' Cyn hastened to intervene; this conversation was utterly pointless in the circumstances—and highly embarrassing! 'Wolf and I met again by accident, not design—on the part of either of us!' Neither of them could possibly have known the circumstances in which they would meet again!

Roger still frowned. 'An accidental meeting he didn't hesitate to take full advantage of.' He looked at Wolf disparagingly.

'As you didn't hesitate to take advantage of the situation seven years ago!' Wolf accused harshly, his eyes narrowed to steely slits now, his mouth a thin line, his body taut as he sat forward in his seat.

'I was around to pick up the pieces, yes,' Roger acknowledged coldly.

'Men like you make me sick!' Wolf rasped disgustedly.

'And men like you——'

'I said stop this!' Cyn cut in with impatient incredulity, glaring at both of them. 'I'm not some choice bone the two of you can wrangle over,' she snapped. 'And what both of you seem to have forgotten is that I'm an adult, with a mind of my own, and I can make what decisions and choices that I please. And it *pleases* me at the moment for both of you to shut up!' She was breathing hard in her agitation. 'You I am driving back to town as soon as I'm washed and dressed,' she told Wolf forcefully. 'And you,' she turned to Roger now, 'I'll talk to about this when you're in a more reasonable frame of mind. This is not the time to do it,' she added with a pointed look in Wolf's direction; he had been nothing but deliberately provoking since Roger's arrival.

'I couldn't agree more.' Roger stood up abruptly, putting down his undrunk mug of coffee. 'If you need me you know where I am.' He moved to kiss Cyn briefly on the cheek. 'And if you allow yourself to become involved with him again then you surely will need me!' he added grimly, looking at her pityingly as he shook his head.

Wolf stood up too, his mouth twisted scornfully. 'Is that how you manage to stay in Cyn's life, Collins?' he taunted. 'By always being around to "pick up the pieces"?'

'You bastard!' Cyn reacted instinctively, her hand arcing up as her fingers made sharp contact with Wolf's cheek. A loud crack sounded in the otherwise silence of the room, and a livid mark already started to appear on that rigidly clenched cheek even as Cyn's hand dropped limply back to her side. Only Wolf had ever been able to evoke such violent emotions in her!

'Continue to think of him in that way, Cyn,' Roger warned grimly. 'Because that's exactly what he is!'

Cyn was mortified at her own actions, staring in horrified fascination at Wolf's face as his cheek continued to change colour, the imprint of her fingers showing white now against his otherwise tanned complexion.

Wolf said nothing, just continued to meet her gaze for long timeless minutes before finally turning to look at the other man. 'I believe you said you were leaving...?' he said pointedly.

Cyn gasped at his arrogance. Although why she should feel in the least surprised by it, she didn't know; she surely hadn't imagined her instinctive reaction to his deliberate baiting of Roger would have made any difference to his dislike of the other man!

'This is my home, Wolf,' she reminded him tightly. 'And Roger is more welcome in it than you are. At any time!' She glared at him.

His brows rose tauntingly. 'And yet I'm the one who just spent the night here with you,' he said softly—challengingly.

Cyn gasped again, at the unmistakable implication in his words this time; they both knew he hadn't spent the night 'with' her, and yet it was the impression he was determined to give Roger. 'You——'

'Cyn always was a fool where you're concerned,' Roger answered him coldly, hands clenched at his sides. 'But I hope she'll be the one to tell you where to go this time.' He looked fiercely at Cyn, willing her to do just that.

'He can go to hell for all I care!' Her cheeks were flushed in her anger as she glared at Wolf.

His mouth quirked wryly. 'And back,' he acknowledged mockingly. 'Too late, Cyn; I've already been there,' he said harshly, his eyes glacial now. 'And I have no intention of going back!'

'You——'

'I think it's time I left you two to argue this out amongst yourselves,' Roger cut in grimly, moving to grasp the top of Cyn's arms in his hands. 'Don't make the mistake of thinking he's changed, Cyn,' he pleaded gently, his gaze holding hers. 'Because he'll try to destroy you all over again.' He shook his head wearily.

She knew he was right; she also knew that Wolf didn't even have to try, that he could do it all too easily just by being in her life at all. That was why he had to be *out* of it, as soon as possible!

'He's leaving, Roger,' she assured him firmly. 'Right now.'

'Well, as soon as she's got some clothes on, anyway,' Wolf put in softly.

Cyn turned on him fiercely, filled with rage at the mocking arch of his brows as he returned her gaze. 'Perhaps you'd better go, Roger,' she told him tightly, her gaze never wavering from Wolf's. 'What I have to say to Wolf would be better done without an audience!' She could tell him exactly what she thought of him—and his innuendoes!—once they were completely alone!

Roger squeezed her arms before releasing her. 'I'll call you,' he promised gruffly, not even sparing Wolf another glance before going, and the cottage door closed softly behind him.

A pin could have been heard to drop in the silence that followed his departure—not the sewing kind, but the pin of a hand-grenade, before the big explosion! Because Cyn didn't doubt that was what was about to happen—because *she* intended being the one to cause it!

Her eyes glittered deeply violet as she turned to look at Wolf, those eyes widening with deepening anger as he limped over to a chair before sinking down into it weakly, the pained expression back on his face. 'Don't try and evoke my sympathy in an effort to stop me throwing you out of here,' she snapped incredulously. 'After that display you just put on for Roger's benefit, I ought to make you walk all the way back to town!'

Wolf sank back wearily, his eyes closing for several seconds before he looked across at her once again. 'That's exactly what it was, Cyn,' he grated harshly. 'A display. If Collins had stayed any longer I'd probably have collapsed at his feet,' he disclosed grimly.

Cyn's expression didn't alter. 'And after the completely erroneous impression you just tried to give him I'd probably have left you there!' she scorned.

'I don't doubt it,' he nodded abruptly.

'What did you think you were doing?' she demanded impatiently. 'Isn't it enough that Roger knew about the two of us seven years ago, without leading him to believe——'

'We were engaged seven years ago,' rasped Wolf, sitting forward tautly. 'Why the hell shouldn't he have known about us?'

'That isn't what I meant, and you know it,' she said exasperatedly. 'He knows how we broke up. And why. To deliberately give him the impression that there's something between us again now was——'

'Of course he knows the reason we broke up, Cyn.' Wolf was on his feet again now, and moving towards her, a determined glint in his golden eyes. 'He was predominant in it!' he grated harshly as he stood in front of her. 'If it hadn't been for Collins——'

'I would have had no one seven years ago!' Cyn glared up at him. 'He was there for me, Wolf, when you——'

'When I couldn't be!' he finished grimly. 'But I'm here now, Cyn——'

'Not for long!' she scorned. 'I told you, as soon as I'm dressed I'm driving you back to town. I don't care where, as long as it's away from here!'

But Wolf no longer seemed to be listening to her, her reminder that she had to get dressed seeming to have drawn his attention to the fact that she stood in front of him wearing only a thin silky robe over an equally thin silky nightshirt. And at the same time he became aware of it, she was sure, she could feel the thrust of her breasts against that silky material, her anger having made the nipples pert and inviting.

But not to him, she protested inwardly, even as he reached out, with hands that shook slightly, and gently untied the belt at her slender waist, smoothing the material over her shoulders so that the robe slid down her arms before falling to the floor. Cyn stood before him wearing only the pale lilac nightshirt now, her breath caught in her throat, the protest along with it as her gaze was caught and held by his.

'Cyn...!'

It was all he said—but it was enough. Cyn's own pent-up longing and need were also in that aching groan, the scene of the last few minutes only seeming to have heightened those emotions, not deadened them, as she would have wished, and it was desire now raging through her body rather than anger, a desire that burned as strong and fierce as her anger had minutes ago, making her sway weakly towards Wolf and the pleasure she knew to be found in his arms.

Her acquiescence was all the encouragement Wolf needed. His breath released in a sigh of his own rising desire before his head bent and his mouth moved to cover her own.

This had always been so right between them, never any doubts whatsoever that physically they were perfectly attuned, mouths sipping and tasting, tongues dancing a pattern that deepened their desire.

'God... Oh, God...!' Wolf groaned in husky need as his body hardened and moved against Cyn's, his hands sliding down her shoulders now to move to the front of her nightshirt, slowly releasing the buttons even as he continued to kiss her with slow, drugging thoroughness.

Cyn knew she was trapped, not just by the strength of Wolf's desire for her, but by her own burning need for him. And it was a need she badly needed to assuage, curling deep inside her, longing to be set free.

Her hands seemed to move of their own volition, unbuttoning his shirt with less than dexterous movements, the trembling of her hands increasing as she felt the hardness of his skin beneath the thin material, the damp swirl of the hair on his chest.

'Yes, Cyn,' Wolf encouraged as she seemed to hesitate at the intimacy, one of his hands moving up to press hers against him. 'Don't stop now!' he pleaded, his eyes glowing golden as he looked down at her.

Cyn wasn't sure she would be able to even if she wanted to—and she was very afraid she didn't want to! As he stepped closer to her, the warmth of his chest coming into burning contact with the nakedness of her breasts, Cyn forgot everything else but that, and knew herself totally lost. She pushed herself closer against him now, her arms encircling his neck, her breasts crushed against his hardness, the near-pain almost as pleasurable as his mouth on hers.

A moment later the silky material of her nightshirt joined her robe on the carpeted floor, and she stood against him completely naked, groaning deep in her throat as Wolf's hands moved surely to the tips of her breasts, the pad of his thumbs caressing those turgid nipples, heated pleasure instantly coursing through her body, a deep warmth between her thighs.

Wolf's mouth left hers now to travel down the length of her throat, and he dropped to his knees in front of her even as his mouth claimed the thrusting fire of one sensitised nipple in the warm cavern of his mouth, his tongue moving moistly over the hardened tip even as he gently suckled.

Cyn's back arched as she cradled the back of Wolf's head with hands that shook, entangling her fingers in the thickness of his hair as she held him to her, her knees feeling weak with reaction, so that she feared she too might fall to the carpeted floor.

As Wolf pulled her down beside him she didn't have to worry about that any more, but watched with languid eyes as he threw off the last of his clothes, his body lean and hard, before he moved to lie gently on top of her, her thighs cupping his hardness, but not completing their joining, Wolf's hands cradling either side of her face as he looked deeply into her eyes before his mouth claimed hers yet again.

He didn't move, except for his mouth against hers; the kiss went on and on, but Cyn could feel her own need for him burning out of control, her longing for something more, her own hands moving restlessly over the sculptured planes of his body, his flesh hard beneath her touch. 'Wolf, please!' she wrenched her mouth away from his to cry when she could stand no more of the torment, her thighs moving restlessly against the hardness of his.

He raised his head to look down at her, his eyes glowing like molten gold. 'Do you want me, Cyn?' he groaned huskily. 'Tell me you want me!'

How could he doubt it? Every muscle, every nerve-ending, was crying out her need of him.

'Show me, Cyn,' he encouraged hoarsely as he saw the answer in her face. 'Show me that this hasn't changed between us!'

How could it have done? She still felt the same way about him, still loved him, still——

'No!' He moved up above her again in protest as he saw the tears in her eyes now. 'I want you, Cyn,' he told her desperately. 'Every time I see you, I want you. It was always that way between us; I only had to see you to want you, to want to be with you, inside you, making you mine in the one way I knew I could possess you. I want you that way now, Cyn,' he groaned as he raised himself above her, poised there, waiting for her to complete the act.

Which she did without hesitation, wanting him in the same way, raising her hips to meet his, instantly feeling his bold hardness entering her warm softness, still for a moment as they adjusted to the intimacy, before he began to move against her in a rhythm as old as time, as strong as the oceans—and as totally out of control!

It had always been this way between them, nothing measured or calculated, but a fierce rushing tide that swept them both in its path, their movements perfectly matched even as that fierceness grew and grew to a crescendo that threatened to drown them both, but in a tide of ecstasy.

Cyn's nails dug into the tautness of Wolf's back as she felt her body tighten with pleasure with each stroke of his hardness within her, feeling Wolf's control starting to break even as her own tension rose and then shattered into a thousand pieces, taking her along with it as wave after wave of trembling ecstasy claimed her. Wolf cried her name into the warm cavern of her throat as he felt her earth-shattering spasms along the length of his body, tensing one final time before joining her in that shuddering climax that seemed pleasurably never-ending.

But it did come to an end, and when it did Cyn became fully aware of the sprawled nakedness of their bodies as they lay on the carpeted floor, the weight of Wolf's body still above her, their thighs still intimately entwined.

She lay in stunned disbelief at what had just happened between them. Minutes ago—she had no idea how many, time seemed unimportant when she was with Wolf like this!—she had been blazingly angry with Wolf, determined to get him away from her cottage, and out of her life. And now this. It was unbelievable!

Although... perhaps not so unbelievable as it might seem, she consoled herself with an inward groan. Anger was as fierce an emotion as desire—and Wolf had always brought out the deepest of emotions in her!

He raised his head from resting against the dampness of her breasts as he felt the small protesting movement she involuntarily made. As he saw the pained expression in her deeply violet-coloured eyes the pleasure slowly faded from his own taut features, a dark frown furrowing his brow as he looked down at her. 'We didn't do anything wrong, Cyn,' he told her gruffly, shaking his head.

Didn't do anything wrong! They hadn't been suited seven years ago, let alone now, and until yesterday Wolf had been about to marry someone else; how could he say that their having made love wasn't wrong? It had certainly been wrong for her!

She pushed at his chest, and at last he moved away from her, at least freeing her from that intimacy, although she was left with one equally devastating. Both of them were still completely naked, the bright sunlight streaming through the windows clearly showing the tanned beauty of Wolf's body as he got slowly to his feet.

Cyn scrambled to her own feet, grabbing up her robe as she did so, her cheeks fiery red as she pulled it on under Wolf's watchful gaze. 'You——' She broke off as she heard the sound of a car in the driveway, her expression instantly panic-stricken. Who else could be calling on her on a Sunday morning? Unless it was Roger come back for some reason?

Wolf had heard the arrival of the car outside too, and moved with a lithe grace to look out of one of the tiny front windows, uncaring of his nakedness. 'Gerald,' he said harshly as he turned back to look at Cyn, his expression grimly accusing. 'The men in your life seem to be falling over each other today, don't they?' he scorned.

Gerald Harcourt here?

Now?

When she and Wolf had just——

Oh, God!

CHAPTER NINE

'DON'T stand there making accusations that, in the circumstances, can only be totally ridiculous,' Cyn told Wolf impatiently, even as she frantically began to gather up his discarded clothing. 'I doubt very much if Gerald is here to see me at all!' She thrust the crumpled clothes at him, glaring at him as he made no effort to put any of them on: Gerald would be out of his car and knocking on the door any second now. She just hoped he didn't glance in the window first! 'Wolf!' she prompted worriedly, shooting anxious glances towards the door.

He at least moved away from the window, although he still made no move to put his clothes back on. 'What do you mean, you doubt Gerald is here to see you? This is your home——'

'And until yesterday *you* were going to marry Gerald's daughter,' Cyn reminded him distractedly, moving the curtain slightly aside to glance out of the window herself now. Gerald was climbing out of his car into the sunshine, a frown marring his brow as he looked at Wolf's BMW parked in the driveway in front of his car. 'He knows you're here, Wolf.' She dropped the curtain back into place before turning back to look at Wolf; he still hadn't made any effort to dress. 'If you aren't going to put those on,' she indicated the clothes in his hand, 'then at least have the decency to take yourself back upstairs to the bedroom so that Gerald can't see you!'

Wolf still scowled. 'I don't give a damn whether he sees me or not——'

'But I do!' Cyn glared at him. 'If you care anything for me at all, Wolf, you'll go upstairs,' she added in a steely voice. He may not care for himself, but God knew what Gerald was going to think of her, ignorant of their past relationship as he was—and she doubted if he would remain around long enough to be *given* an explanation of that once he had seen Wolf's nakedness and drawn his own conclusions!

Wolf's expression darkened even more. 'Of course I care about you!' he rasped. 'I've just made love to you! What sort of man do you think I am——?'

'I really don't know any more, Wolf,' she said wearily as she heard the sound of Gerald's footsteps on the gravel pathway outside. 'The sort that isn't going to humiliate me in front of Rebecca's father, I hope.' She was willing him to go up the stairs now, her hands tightly clenched at her sides. *She* had just made love with him too, and was still badly shaken by the experience—couldn't he see that?

'Rebecca's father,' Wolf repeated softly. 'Is that really how you think of him?'

'Of course I—— Oh God, Wolf, not now!' she groaned as Gerald's knock sounded on the door. 'Please!'

For long, timeless seconds he didn't move, and then with an abrupt nod he turned and went into the kitchen— taking his clothes with him, thank God! Cyn looked about the sitting-room anxiously for anything he might have left behind, spotting her silky nightshirt partially hidden under the chair, moving to push it completely under the piece of furniture before going to the door to answer Gerald's second—more forceful?—knock; he knew the two of them were here by the two vehicles parked outside, must wonder what was keeping them.

Cyn tightened the belt to her robe more securely about her waist, pushing the blond tangle of her hair back from her face; she prayed that Gerald would think her bedraggled appearance was due to the fact that she had just got out of bed, and not because she and Wolf had just made abandoned love on the sitting-room floor!

Her cheeks flamed with colour just at the memory of it, the two high spots of colour burning there as she finally opened the door. 'Gerald!' She tried to sound pleased as well as surprised as she smiled up at him.

His returning smile was only half-hearted, and he looked as if he hadn't slept all night; there were lines of weariness about his eyes, making him look all of his forty-three years today. 'I tried to telephone you earlier, but your telephone seems to be out of order...' He looked at her questioningly, making no effort to enter the cottage, even though Cyn had opened the door wider for him to do so.

Not that she could exactly blame him for his wariness; he must wonder what Wolf's car was doing parked outside her cottage! 'A slight accident with the connection, I'm afraid,' she said dismissively. 'I have to call an engineer to come out and fix it. Do come in, Gerald,' she invited lightly. 'The breeze is cooler than you imagine.' She gave a strained laugh as that very same errant breeze blew against her robe to sweep the silky material to one side to reveal the long length of her naked thighs before she had a chance to catch hold of it.

Gerald had the good sense to duck as he entered the cottage, although he frowned a little as he saw the odd layout of her sitting-room, with the furniture all back against the walls.

Cyn's cheeks blushed anew as she remembered that minutes ago she and Wolf had made love in the very spot Gerald was now standing. 'Excuse the mess, Gerald,' she said awkwardly. 'But I——'

'It's my fault, I'm afraid,' Wolf cut in smoothly as he came through from the kitchen—fully dressed now, Cyn was relieved to see!—leaning heavily on the crutches that he hadn't felt in need of earlier this morning.

'What on earth——!' Gerald looked dumbfounded as he took in the crutches and Wolf's bandaged ankle.

Cyn stared at Wolf too, wondering what he was going to say in answer to the other man's obvious curiosity.

'I drove down to see Miss Smith yesterday in the hope that she could be of further help concerning Rebecca,' he told Gerald confidently. 'And while I was here I fell over her telephone wire, totally destroying the connection,' he dismissed briskly, 'and injuring my ankle into the bargain,' he grimaced self-derisively.

The truth, of course, Cyn realised ruefully; she should have realised Wolf wouldn't be thrown by the other man's arrival, as *she* was. And why should he be? What he had just said was the truth; it was what had happened after that he was never likely to tell the other man!

Gerald looked down concernedly at Wolf's ankle. 'Is it broken?'

'No, just badly sprained,' Wolf dismissed lightly. 'But it meant I couldn't drive back to town last night.'

Cyn could see the question forming in Gerald's eyes; then why hadn't Cyn driven him back!

'Of course, Cyn offered to drive me back to town.' Wolf was way ahead of him, once again his voice was smoothly unconcerned. 'But you know the state of my mother's health,' he shrugged in Gerald's direction. 'It was impossible for me to go there.'

'Yes... Yes, of course,' Gerald acknowledged with a frown.

'And Cyn kindly offered to let me stay here until I felt a little more mobile,' Wolf smiled his thanks at her, only the hardness of his gaze belying his gratitude. 'Any more news where Rebecca's concerned?' He turned sharply towards the other man.

'Ah.' Gerald seemed momentarily caught off guard, shifting uncomfortably as he returned Wolf's gaze.

There *was* more news, that much was obvious, and, knowing what she did of the situation, Cyn could hazard a guess as to what it was. Although the change of subject did seem to have successfully diverted Gerald's attention away from the fact that Wolf had known where she lived at all. Because he shouldn't have done, not in the normal course of events!

'Coffee,' she said decisively. 'I think we could all do with some,' she explained as the two men turned to look at her. 'And some toast too,' she added firmly. Meals seemed to be becoming a thing of the past since Wolf had arrived here yesterday!

His eyes were narrowed on her questioningly, as if he sensed her prevarication. 'Coffee and toast sounds good,' he nodded slowly, watching Cyn speculatively now as she met his gaze with deliberate innocence. 'I need to take one of my painkilling tablets, anyway,' he added thoughtfully.

'Gerald?' Cyn turned thankfully to the other man now. The strain in his face seemed to have increased since the subject of Rebecca had been reintroduced. Oh, dear, the news didn't look good at all, Cyn realised with an inner grimace.

'Thank you,' he accepted gravely. 'I have to admit, breakfast was the furthest thing from my mind this morning, after——' He broke off awkwardly, as if re- alising he had once again brought up a subject that would probably be best left alone until they had all had something to eat and drink. 'Coffee and toast sounds wonderful,' he smiled at Cyn gratefully before sitting down. 'I'm sorry, Wolf.' He instantly jumped up again as he saw the other man's struggle to cope with the crutches and sit down in the chair at the same time. 'Can I be of any assistance?'

Considering Wolf had been managing perfectly well without the aid of the crutches not half an hour ago, Cyn decided to leave the two men to it, escaping into the kitchen even as Gerald crossed to Wolf's side to help him into the chair.

It was the first privacy she had had to realise the enormity of what had happened between herself and Wolf this morning, and her own strain showed as she leaned heavily against one of the kitchen units, unable yet to even think about getting them all some breakfast, let alone actually doing it! She and Wolf had made love, right there, on the sitting-room floor...!

And it had been just the same between them as it always was, the instantaneous response to each other, that same earth-shattering pleasure, the mindless release that only they could give each other. At least...that only *Wolf* could give *her*. Because there had been no other men in her life in that intimate sense. She wondered now, with unreasonable jealousy—unreasonable, because what had happened between them had been completely unexpected—how many other women there had been for Wolf during the last seven years. Besides Barbara, of course...

Barbara. It always came back to the other woman. Why, oh, why didn't he just marry Barbara and leave all other women alone?

It was unfair, totally unfair. Cyn's body was still aching, pleasurably, from the ecstasy Wolf had given her. And must never give her again! She wouldn't, couldn't fall into that trap a second time. She had freed herself from it once, and she mustn't go willingly into it again. Then unwillingly? She was never unwilling with Wolf, that was the trouble, she acknowledged with a self-disgusted groan.

'Need any help?' Gerald offered from close behind her.

Cyn spun round guiltily, sure that guilt must be plainly written on the paleness of her cheeks. 'I didn't hear you come in,' she weakly excused her over-reaction. 'And no, I think I can manage fine on my own—thank you,' she added awkwardly, the brief smile that curved her lips nowhere near reaching the dark distress of her eyes. 'Please go back into the sitting-room and join Wolf—er—Mr Thornton,' she amended awkwardly as she remembered the relationship she and Wolf were supposed to have.

He grimaced. 'I think I'd rather stay out here and help you!'

Cyn had to smile, in spite of herself. 'Safer, hmm?' she guessed ruefully, putting the coffee on to percolate—they were probably all going to be in need of something stronger than the instant kind before the morning was through!

'For the moment,' Gerald acknowledged. 'Let me do that.' He took over the making of the coffee and putting the mugs on the tray while Cyn put the bread in to toast.

She didn't press him. She didn't have to, could already guess, more or less, what it was he was going to tell them. And he was right, it could wait.

'I had no idea you were so domesticated, Gerald,' Wolf remarked derisively when the other man carried the laden tray through to the sitting-room.

Cyn shot him a reproving look as she carried the coffee-table over to place it in front of him so that Gerald could put the tray down. 'Sugar?' she enquired with sarcasm as she sat down to pour the coffee; his mood could certainly do with sweetening up!

Her dig wasn't wasted on him. His brows arched. 'Just black, as usual, thanks,' he drawled mockingly.

As usual, Cyn noted, her mouth tightening, deliberately not meeting his taunting gaze as she handed him his coffee. Why did she bother wasting her time verbally fencing with him? She always came out the loser!

'So, Gerald,' he turned to the other man once they all had a mug of coffee and had helped themselves to the buttered toast, 'what do you have to tell me that was so important you came looking for me here instead of waiting until I got back to town? Although,' he added with a frown, 'I don't exactly remember your ever saying you *had* come here to see me...' He looked at the other man with questioningly raised brows.

'I didn't,' Gerald told him bluntly. 'I actually came to see Cyn for the same reason you did; to see if there was anything else she could tell me concerning Rebecca's—disappearance.'

'I see,' Wolf acknowledged softly. 'And was there?'

Gerald frowned at the question. 'I haven't had a chance to ask her yet.' He shook his head a little dazedly at Wolf's obvious antagonism.

Cyn felt quite sorry for Gerald at this moment, but was powerless to help him, knowing as she did that Wolf was motivated by so much more than Rebecca's disappearance. In fact, in the circumstances, she thought it was best if she just stayed out of the conversation altogether!

But Wolf had other ideas! 'Then ask away,' he invited hardly. 'I was just under the impression you'd been in the kitchen together so long you must have already discussed it,' he added harshly, his gaze narrowed on them both.

'We were too busy preparing the food.' Cyn was the one to hurriedly answer him; really, he was starting to sound like a jealous lover, something they both knew he wasn't! 'And I'm afraid I can't add anything to what I've already told you about Rebecca,' she shrugged dismissively.

'Can't—or won't?' Wolf put in softly, his gaze speculative now.

'Can't,' she answered firmly; she had no intention of breaking Rebecca's confidence to her. But at the same time, she felt the warmth enter her cheeks, and knew it must make her look guilty. But if her supposition about Gerald was correct, there was no need for her to become involved in the finer details of Rebecca's decision not to marry Wolf. *If* her supposition was correct.

'Fair enough,' Gerald accepted with a sigh. 'You may as well know, Wolf,' he continued heavily, 'Rebecca telephoned me this morning. It seems that when she decided to go away to think she—didn't go alone,' the last came out in a rush, as if he was anxious to get this over with now that he had started. 'I'm so sorry, Wolf,' he groaned awkwardly, 'but it seems Rebecca has been— seeing young Glen Reynolds!'

Glen. So that was the gardener's name. Mmm, it somehow fitted that golden-god image. Not that his parents could have known when they named him that he was going to look like a tanned—— Oh, lord, she was burbling in her thoughts now! What did it matter what the man's name was? She was sure that wasn't the part that would interest Wolf.

She could hardly bear to look at him. This was the second time in his life his fiancée had walked out on him, and both times, seemingly, into the arms of another man. Seemingly, because in Cyn's case it hadn't really been true. But this time, with Rebecca, it was. What must Wolf be thinking?

It was difficult to tell that from his expression—a closed look in his eyes, his mouth a taut thin line. 'And who,' he spoke quietly, 'is Glen Reynolds?'

Gerald looked more uncomfortable than ever. 'The young chap I have in to take care of my garden,' he revealed reluctantly, an embarrassed grimace on his face as he looked regretfully at Wolf.

Cyn looked at him too, trying to decipher his reaction to this piece of information. Once again it was difficult to tell. His expression was enigmatic, although there was a certain tension to his body that hadn't been there seconds ago. Cyn might almost have felt sorry for him—if she hadn't known that he still had Barbara in his life.

'I had no idea, Wolf,' Gerald hurried on awkwardly as Wolf made no response to the disclosure. 'If I had I would have intervened——'

'Why?' Wolf frowned, eyes narrowed.

Gerald looked disconcerted. 'Why?' he repeated dazedly, moving his shoulders uncomfortably. 'Well, because——'

'Yes?' Wolf prompted softly.

'Well, I—— Good God, man, he's the gardener!' Gerald exclaimed incredulously. 'Of course I would have tried to put a stop to it. What can he and Rebecca possibly have in common?' he dismissed scathingly.

Wolf's mouth twisted. 'Strange, I've never thought of you as a snob, Gerald,' he murmured mockingly.

The older man flushed. 'It has nothing to do with being a snob,' he snapped, uncomfortable with the barb. 'But Rebecca's my only child; of course I want the best for her!'

Wolf gave an abrupt inclination of his head. 'Is that why you encouraged her to marry me?'

'Of course. She wasn't exactly an unwilling victim, Wolf!' Gerald defended as he realised he had fallen into the verbal trap the other man had set for him. 'Rebecca's always liked you, you know that. Damn it, she *wanted* to marry you!' he added exasperatedly as Wolf just continued to look at him, his brows raised.

'Wanted, Gerald. Past tense,' Wolf nodded grimly. 'And now, as is a woman's prerogative, she's changed her mind. For whatever reason,' he added dismissively. 'As long as she's all right, and with this young man we presume she can come to no harm, I don't see——'

'No harm!' Gerald repeated incredulously. 'She's staying God knows where, with young Reynolds, and you don't think she can come to any harm!' His voice rose in his agitation.

'Gerald, Rebecca's over eighteen, she went with him willingly,' Wolf drawled derisively. 'I don't see that there's a lot any of us can do,' he shrugged.

'*The two of you were getting married*!' Gerald stood up to glare down at Wolf.

Wolf nodded calmly. 'And now Rebecca's decided she doesn't want to get married after all. At least, not to me,' he added drily.

'But what about you?' Gerald demanded angrily. 'If you really loved Rebecca you wouldn't let her go this easily,' he accused, hands clenched at his sides.

Wolf shrugged. 'I care for Rebecca—very much. And I'm sure we would have had a reasonably happy marriage, based on that caring we had for each other. But I'm certainly not going to run after her like some lovesick schoolboy, if that's what you mean,' he added harshly, a hard glitter in the gold of his eyes. 'If it's Reynolds she wants, then I wish her well,' he finished.

Cyn listened to the exchange without contributing to it. What could she say that would in any way alleviate the tension that now existed between the two men? Besides, Wolf's attitude to Rebecca walking out on him was too painfully reminiscent of the way he had reacted seven years ago when she had told him *she* wasn't going to marry him!

'Well, I damn well don't!' Gerald told him furiously. 'You may not have any interest in stopping Rebecca making the biggest mistake of her life, but I certainly do!'

'She's your daughter,' Wolf acknowledged softly.

'She was *your* fiancée!' Gerald reminded him accusingly. 'For what that was obviously worth. God, why am I bothering with this?' he sighed his impatience with Wolf's indifference. 'You obviously aren't interested any more in what happens to Rebecca, and——' He broke off abruptly, suddenly still, a slowly dawning comprehension on his face as he looked first at Wolf, then at Cyn, her face starting to burn at the speculation she saw in his gaze, before he turned back to Wolf, a contemptuous twist to his lips now. 'What kind of fool have I been?' he said slowly. 'Just how serious is the injury to your ankle, Wolf?' He looked at the other man suspiciously.

In answer to that Wolf stood up, without the aid of the crutches, putting his weight on both feet, just as if there had never been a sprain to his ankle at all. Damn him!

'*That* serious,' Gerald realised self-disgustedly, turning to look at Cyn now. 'I'm surprised at you, Cyn,' he said disappointedly. 'No, stunned would be a more appropriate word to describe how I feel right now,' he added, shaking his head dazedly. 'I can't really take any of this in,' he frowned.

'There's nothing to take in,' Cyn hastened to assure him, her gaze pleading. 'Wolf really did injure his ankle, and if you'd seen him last night you'd know exactly why I didn't take him back to town then——'

'The same can hardly be said about this morning, Cyn,' Wolf was the one to put in drily.

She turned to glare at him. 'There's hardly been time to drive you anywhere this morning, what with Roger's visit earlier, and then——'

'Yes?' Wolf prompted mockingly as she broke off abruptly, her face colouring brightly red as she remembered all too vividly what had happened 'then'.

How she hated him at that moment—him and the fact that he was deliberately humiliating her in front of Gerald. And why? Because he wanted to save his own pride after being rejected by Rebecca!

'You can go back to town with Gerald!' she realised with a feeling of deep relief at the thought of not having to spend any more time alone in his company herself. 'I'm sure the two of you still have a lot to talk about, and what better opportunity to do that than on the drive back to London?' Now that the idea had taken root, and grown, she was feeling quite pleased with herself for her stroke of genius. Of course Wolf could go back to town with Gerald, it was the perfect solution.

Wolf didn't look as if it was. The dark scowl was back on his face now, a dangerous glitter in his eyes as he glared at her for making the suggestion. 'I hadn't intended returning to town—just yet,' he told her harshly. 'I think we're the ones who still have a lot to talk about.'

Cyn couldn't even look at Gerald as he still watched the two of them speculatively. 'I've already told you, Wolf, if you and Rebecca should change your mind about your wedding and decide to go ahead with it after all, I'll be pleased to talk to both of you concerning the arrangements, otherwise I think our—business together is concluded.' She met his gaze challengingly, willing him to go now. She desperately needed to be alone now, to gather her battered pride—and defences!—back together.

'Do you?' Wolf returned softly, his hard gaze raking over her mercilessly now. Endlessly, it seemed, as Cyn squirmed under the onslaught. 'Perhaps you're right,' he said decisively, turning to look at Gerald. 'Can you give me a lift back to my flat?'

There was no doubting that Gerald could, it was whether he *would* that was the question! After Wolf's deliberate baiting of Cyn the other man couldn't doubt that more had happened here this weekend between her and Wolf than either of them seemed prepared to say at the moment, and, considering what Wolf's relationship had been to Gerald's daughter until yesterday, the older man would be perfectly within his rights to feel outraged at what he thought might have happened!

Cyn looked at Gerald too as they waited for his answer, a silent pleading in her eyes. He frowned as he saw that plea, obviously puzzled as to the exact relationship that had apparently developed—literally overnight, to his unknowing eyes!—between his daughter's fiancé and the woman he had asked to help that very same daughter with her wedding arrangements.

But with one last probing look at Cyn he turned and nodded to Wolf. 'Perhaps we *could* use that time to talk,' he accepted gravely. 'If you're ready to go now...?'

Wolf nodded abruptly. 'There doesn't seem to be any reason to stay,' he rasped harshly. 'If you wouldn't mind waiting in the car for me?'

Gerald looked as if he minded very much! 'I'll be outside,' he told the other man with a curt nod. 'Goodbye, Cyn,' he added with abrupt finality, barely glancing in her direction before leaving, and the cottage door closed with quiet force behind him.

The silence in the room after his departure was so strained that Cyn felt like screaming, her hands twisting together in front of her as she forced herself to raise her neck and look at Wolf. Granite—rock-hewn granite. That was what his face looked as if it were carved from; his expression was coldly forbidding.

Cyn fell back on the only defence she could muster; her own anger towards him for the things he had said in front of Gerald. 'There was no need for any of that,' she snapped, shaking her head disgustedly.

He looked unmoved. 'Wasn't there?' he returned icily.

She frowned across at him, her gaze searching. He had achieved nothing by giving Gerald the impression that there was a relationship between them, except to alienate Gerald from him—— And her, she realised, her eyes widening with disbelief as she knew *that* was what he had set out to do! He hadn't believed her when she told him there was nothing between herself and Gerald, or at least, if he had believed her, he had now made sure there never *would* be anything between them. He could still do something like that, even after——!

'Get out, Wolf,' she told him wearily. 'Just get out.'

'Not until you've answered one question for me,' he ground out harshly.

As far as Cyn was concerned, she didn't think he was in any position to make conditions. But she felt too sick at this moment to argue with him. 'What is it?' she sighed heavily.

His mouth twisted. 'You knew about Rebecca and this man Reynolds, didn't you?'

It was so far from what she had been expecting the question to be that she gasped her surprise, frowning at him as he watched her with narrowed eyes. She moistened her lips, swallowing hard as she saw the angry glitter in those golden eyes. 'I——'

'You knew,' he said disgustedly as he saw the guilt in her face, his hands clenching at his sides.

'Yes, I knew there was someone,' she answered defensively. 'Not his name, or anything like that, but I knew he worked for Gerald.'

Wolf's mouth tightened. 'And yet when I arrived here yesterday, and asked you if Rebecca had told you anything else during her telephone call to you, you told me she hadn't!'

Cyn shook her head, meeting his gaze challengingly. 'I said I'd told you everything she *asked* me to.'

'But not everything you knew,' Wolf realised self-derisively, the twisted smile on his lips owing nothing to humour. 'Well, now we all know,' he scorned. 'And I know once and for all just what sort of woman you are!'

Cyn swallowed convulsively. 'And what sort of woman is that, Wolf?' she prompted reluctantly, dreading—and yet needing to know!—the answer.

He looked at her coldly. 'The sort of woman who's so bitter and twisted about what happened between us seven years ago that——'

'That isn't true!' Cyn gasped protestingly.

'—that you'd do anything to get back at me!' Wolf finished harshly, every muscle and sinew in his body tense with controlled fury. 'Is that what this morning was about too? Did you hope to throw my own weakness where you're concerned back in my face, once we'd made love?' he demanded disgustedly. 'What a pity Gerald arrived when he did and spoilt the moment for you!'

Cyn looked at him disbelievingly. He couldn't really believe what he was saying? And yet she could see by the bitter twist to his own mouth that he did, that it was the only way he could think of to explain what had happened between them this morning. And wasn't it better if he *did* think that, rather than the truth; that she still loved him!

She turned away so that he shouldn't see the sheen of tears in her eyes. 'Think what you like, Wolf,' she told him huskily. 'Just leave me alone.'

'Oh, I intend to,' he assured her hardly. 'I'll send someone down to collect my car, so don't worry that the two of us need ever see each other again. We've managed to avoid doing exactly that for the last seven years; I don't see why we can't continue to do so!'

Cyn waited until she heard the cottage door slam behind him as he left before she allowed the sobs to rack her body, her face buried in her hands as she cried as though her heart were breaking into a million pieces.

Which it was...

CHAPTER TEN

'No, Rebecca, I really can't,' Cyn told the girl firmly as they sat across the luncheon table from each other.

Rebecca had telephoned the agency only this morning to ask Cyn to meet her in town for lunch because she had something important she wanted to discuss with her, expecting, with her usual youthful arrogance, that Cyn would have nothing better to do than drive up to town to meet her. Cyn had plenty to keep her busy at the moment. The bookings for weddings were gaining momentum now, as she had thought they would. But considering their past relationship, Cyn hadn't felt she could refuse Rebecca's request. Although at this moment she dearly wished she had.

It was over a month since Wolf had walked out of her cottage, a month when, besides the man he had sent down to collect his car and belongings, and the bouquet of flowers she had received from Rebecca, the card accompanying them having the simple message 'Thanks for all your help and understanding', she had heard nothing more of the Harcourt family. Or Wolf...

She certainly hadn't expected her first contact with them again after all that time to be Rebecca asking her to once again help with the wedding arrangements!

Cyn couldn't imagine what had happened during the last month, but Rebecca was glowing with happiness, showing none of the doubts that had been so predominant in her behaviour a month ago, the same doubts that had caused her to flee rather than go through with her marriage to Wolf.

It was apparently all back on again, and Rebecca wanted to re-employ Perfect Bliss to make all the arrangements.

'Does your father know you're talking to me about this?' Cyn asked with a frown. Surely Gerald couldn't be happy about it if he did, not after the impression Wolf had given him that morning at her cottage?

'Of course,' Rebecca answered happily. 'When I told him I was going to give your agency a call, his exact words were, "I don't care who you call, as long as you go through with the wedding this time"!' She grinned. 'As if I wouldn't.' She smiled dreamily.

Cyn looked at her searchingly. There could be no doubting the difference in Rebecca now. Happiness was radiating out of her. But could she really be so sure she was doing the right thing this time around? There was no way Cyn would ever tell the girl what had happened between herself and Wolf a month ago, let alone seven years ago, but it was nevertheless a fact that Wolf had made love to her four weeks ago, and there was still Barbara hovering in the background of his life, like a dark cloud blotting out the sun. And happiness.

'Rebecca, are you sure this time? Really sure?' Cyn frowned.

'Absolutely,' the girl replied without hesitation.

'And Wolf and your father? The last time I saw the two of them they—weren't the best of friends.' Cyn winced at the memory of that conversation.

'Oh, they're fine now,' Rebecca dismissed with a shrug. 'It's business as usual. And Wolf has forgiven me for behaving so stupidly.'

Obviously, Cyn grimaced inwardly. But would Rebecca forgive Wolf if she were to find out what had happened between him and Cyn the weekend she went away to think?

'So much so,' Rebecca continued lightly, 'that he's agreed to be Glen's best man!'

Cyn stared at her uncomprehending. Glen...?

'That was my idea,' Rebecca chattered on happily, completely unaware of Cyn's stunned expression. 'I thought it might be a nice gesture, considering he was so understanding about my breaking off our engagement. Glen thought he was more likely to punch him in the face for even daring to ask, but I assured him Wolf was too much of a gentleman to do that. And I was right!' she grinned, blue eyes glowing. 'Wolf said he'd be happy to be best man if he couldn't be the groom. You see,' Rebecca laughed lightly, 'a gentleman!'

It was *Glen* Rebecca intended marrying? Not Wolf? But Cyn had assumed—— That was the problem, she realised, she *had* assumed—and she had assumed incorrectly!

She was surprised at herself for the feeling of relief that washed over her at learning Wolf wasn't to be Rebecca's husband after all. It shouldn't matter to her what Wolf did with his life now. It shouldn't. But it did...

She had tried to convince herself this last month that she didn't care about Wolf any more, had almost thought she had succeeded—until Rebecca told her the wedding planned for August was back on. Then the pain of realising Wolf was getting married after all had cut through her like a knife, causing an actual physical ache in her chest. And now she learnt that Wolf wasn't the intended bridegroom at all!

She shouldn't feel quite so happy about it; what Wolf did with his life shouldn't matter to her. God, how she wished it didn't!

And the fact that he wasn't Rebecca's intended bridegroom made no difference to the answer she was going to have to give Rebecca. Wolf was going to be the best man at the wedding, and there was no way Cyn could see him in August. Or any other time...

'Your father is all right about Glen now?' she frowned, remembering Gerald's feelings the last time she spoke to him concerning the mere idea of Rebecca being involved with his gardener.

'He is now,' Rebecca grimaced with feeling, showing Cyn that it hadn't been as easy convincing her father about Glen's rightness for her as she would have wished. 'He's offered a loan, and Glen has agreed to accept, so that he can start his own landscape gardening business. As long as it is only a loan; Glen can be very proud, especially when it comes to my father's money. That was why I had so much trouble convincing *Glen* about the two of us in the first place!' she finished disgustedly.

Cyn straightened in her chair. 'I'm glad it's all worked out for you, Rebecca,' she told the girl, genuinely happy for her.

'*But*?' Rebecca grimaced as she sensed what was coming next.

Cyn gave a rueful smile. 'I did warn you in the beginning...' She shrugged. 'I'm afraid things have become rather booked up this last month, and there's just no way I could agree to take on another wedding for August,' she explained lightly, thankful for being able to tell the truth. Oh, if she were really pushed she could probably fit in another wedding—but not one that was going to bring her anywhere near being in contact with Wolf!

Rebecca looked disappointed. 'Then maybe we could put it back to September...' she said doubtfully.

Not September either! 'I'm very flattered, Rebecca,' Cyn smiled ruefully. 'But how do you think Glen would feel about that?' she teased lightly.

'He'd probably agree to wait,' Rebecca laughed. '*I'm* the one who insists on an early wedding; I don't want to give him time to change his mind, or get cold feet!' she admitted candidly.

'As you did,' Cyn reminded her, understanding Gerald's worry that it might happen again. Although she didn't think so; Rebecca was obviously ecstatically happy at the thought of marrying Glen.

'The only reason Glen would change his mind is if his sense of "doing what's right" for me takes over again,' Rebecca grimaced. 'My reasons for running away from the wedding with Wolf were completely different.'

Cyn didn't doubt it, just as she didn't doubt that part of that reason was someone called Barbara... 'Well, as long as it's all worked out now,' she dismissed lightly. 'And I really am pleased for you, Rebecca; I hope you and Glen will be very happy together. I'm only sorry I can't be of help with the arrangements.' Might she be forgiven for the lie! She would have invented a reason why she couldn't be involved in anything that would bring her into contact with Wolf if she didn't have a genuinely truthful one.

'So am I,' Rebecca returned warmly. 'I have a lot to thank you for. I don't know if I'd ever have had the courage to tell my father and Wolf that I didn't want to go through with the wedding, if it hadn't been for your advice.'

Cyn grimaced. 'For God's sake don't tell Wolf that!'

The other girl laughed huskily. 'Formidable, isn't he?' she nodded understandingly, still grinning.

'How is his ankle now?' Cyn voiced casually. 'Better?'

'Completely,' Rebecca nodded. 'Although he's working too hard again,' she added with a frown. 'I may not love him enough to want to marry him, but I do still worry about him. He isn't happy.'

As far as Cyn was concerned she considered Wolf perfectly big enough to take care of himself, and Rebecca's sympathy towards him was completely unnecessary! 'He *has* just lost his fiancée,' she drily reminded the other girl.

Rebecca pulled a face. 'Wolf was no more in love with me in that sense than I was with him—he just decided he wasn't getting any younger, and it was time he got married. And provided a Thornton heir, of course,' she added derisively.

'Very romantic!' Cyn murmured weakly.

'Oh, that isn't really as calculated as it sounds,' Rebecca smiled at Cyn's disgusted expression. 'His brother Alex was killed in an air crash quite a few years ago now. And his wife was never able to have children, which is why, I think, Wolf feels doubly pressured into having some himself,' she explained with a shrug.

It also explained why Wolf and Barbara had never married; Barbara couldn't provide the necessary Thornton heir... At long last Cyn had the answer to the riddle that had puzzled her for so many years.

But it was an answer that brought back her own fear of Wolf. Now, more than ever...

* * *

'I won't be caught out a second time,' Wolf murmured self-derisively as he ducked his head to avoid the low beams as he entered her cottage.

Cyn looked at him dazedly. He was the last person she had expected to see on her doorstep when she went to answer the rap of knuckles on the oak door! She hadn't been in from work long, and had been about to get herself something to eat. But she knew she wasn't going to feel like eating after Wolf had gone! What was he doing here? It couldn't just be coincidence that he had called to see her on the very same evening she had had lunch with Rebecca. What had happened *now* to cause him to come here, when the last time they had met he had made it perfectly plain he never wanted to see her again? She felt herself tensing as she looked across the room at him.

Wolf turned once he reached the unlit fireplace, one dark blond brow raised mockingly at Cyn as she still stood at the open doorway, one of her hands tightly gripping the door. He was still dressed for the office himself, wearing one of those darkly sombre suits Cyn so hated on him. And Rebecca was right; he did look as if he was working too hard, his face drawn and harsh, and he looked as if he might have lost some weight since Cyn last saw him too—— What possible interest was it to her whether he was working too hard or not? Cyn reprimanded herself sharply. What was he doing here?

'Rebecca tells me the two of you had lunch together today,' he finally said, his expression lightly enquiring.

And Cyn wasn't fooled for a moment by this casual approach, eyeing him with suspicion. 'Yes,' she nodded abruptly.

His mouth twisted derisively at her obvious wariness. 'She said you're too busy now in August to help with her wedding arrangements to Glen,' he drawled.

'That's right, I am,' Cyn answered curtly, her tension starting to make the back of her neck ache. 'And if this is a business call, my agency hours of opening are nine till——'

'It isn't a business call, Cyn,' Wolf cut in softly, his eyes narrowed.

Then what was it? Not a social call, certainly! She and Wolf had never been able to indulge in those!

'Rebecca said you asked after me today,' he continued huskily.

'After your health,' Cyn defended, her cheeks feeling warm in her agitation; he made it sound as if she had asked Rebecca for intimate confidences about him! 'Your *ankle*, to be exact,' she snapped.

He gave an acknowledging inclination of his head. 'It's fine again now, thank you.'

'Wolf——'

'When you sent my things back after that weekend, there were some things missing,' he cut easily across her exasperation, his gaze steady now as he watched the heated colour fade from her cheeks, leaving her looking pale—and more wary than ever!

'Things missing . . . ?' she repeated slowly, playing for time, the sick feeling in the pit of her stomach increasing. 'Oh, you mean your painting things?' She tried to sound dismissive. 'You reacted so violently against my having brought them here for you in the first place, I didn't think you'd want them back,' she shrugged lightly, unable to meet his probing gaze.

She shouldn't have kept those things; she knew that she shouldn't at the time. And yet she had been reluctant to let them go; they had belonged to the Wolf she had once known and loved. A Wolf who no longer seemed to exist... But she shouldn't have hung on to those things; they had brought Wolf back into her life once more.

Although it had taken him over a month to decide to come here looking for them...?

She met his gaze head-on now, her head tilted back, blond hair resting silkily against her shoulders. 'Why *don't* you paint any more, Wolf?' she asked bluntly.

He stiffened at the directness of the question, relaxing slightly with effort. 'For the same reason I now run Thornton Industries,' he rasped harshly.

'Money?' she said disbelievingly; she couldn't really believe the Thornton family needed any more of that!

'Of course not——!' He broke off. 'Money has never been important to me, you know that,' he told her gratingly.

Cyn frowned. 'If it isn't important to you, why do you spend all day, every day, making more of it?' She shook her head in puzzlement.

He sighed. 'For the same reason I don't paint any more.'

'We're going round in circles here, Wolf,' Cyn pointed out impatiently.

'You once told me exactly what it was, Cyn,' he said heavily. 'Guilt. And that reasoning hasn't changed.' He drew in a harsh breath. 'I hate running Thornton Industries. I always have. And I always will,' he told her vehemently.

She frowned at him, at the deep fire in his eyes, his fierce expression, the restlessness in his body, that all spoke of his dislike of the shackles that apparently bound him to living a life he disliked intensely. Guilt...? Because of his affair with Alex's wife? Terrible as that had been, it was surely no reason to live a lie, to cut from his life things like happiness and laughter, doing work he enjoyed—more, felt *compelled* to do? Because that was what painting had always meant to him in the past.

'Why the hell are you looking at me like that, Cyn?' he demanded impatiently now. 'You broke off our engagement seven years ago for the very same reason!'

'Seven years, Wolf,' she acknowledged impatiently. 'Plenty of time for you to have changed things. If you'd wanted to,' she added bitterly.

He shook his head, frowning. 'I couldn't bring Alex back.'

'You could have stopped your affair with his wife!' Cyn cried incredulously, breathing hard in her agitation.

Wolf became very still, staring at her. 'What did you say?' he prompted softly.

She shook her head. 'You could have changed your life any time you wanted to, Wolf!' she scorned. 'Instead of which you were about to let history repeat itself, were prepared to bring yet another innocent party into the mess you and Barbara have made of your lives. Thank God Rebecca decided she wanted more from her life than you could obviously give her! Even if she didn't know of your affair with Barbara, she at least knew enough to realise that a marriage between you wouldn't have worked. What a lucky escape both Rebecca *and* I had!' Cyn glared at him.

Wolf stood as if carved from stone, unmoving, unblinking, just staring at Cyn as if he had never seen her before.

Cyn's breasts rose and fell as she breathed agitatedly, each moment that passed increasing her outrage. How dared he come here so that all this could be raked up again? It solved nothing, just brought back all the bitterness and pain. When she so badly needed to start looking forward in her life...

Wolf drew in a shallow breath, seeming to be searching for the right words to say. 'Cyn——'

'I don't know why you came here, Wolf,' she cut in coldly. 'But I wish you'd leave again, and let me at least get on with my life!'

'Cyn, seven years ago you broke our engagement, supposedly, because of what I'd done to Alex.' Wolf ignored her outburst, choosing his words very carefully, a strange new light in his eyes. 'And also, I thought, because you'd realised it was Collins you loved,' he added grimly.

'I've always loved Roger, Wolf,' she retorted. 'He was the family, the brother, I never had!'

Wolf swallowed convulsively, his whole body tense now. 'And is that all he ever was to you?'

'I don't see——'

'Cyn, please!' he grated compellingly, eyes glittering fiercely.

'Yes,' she snapped impatiently. 'That's all he ever was. All he ever could be.' She had never loved anyone but Wolf, not in that way. 'Roger's a homosexual,' she added quietly.

Wolf swallowed again. 'And Alex,' he said slowly. 'Just what did you think I was guilty of where he was concerned seven years ago?'

Her mouth twisted contemptuously. 'I didn't "think" you were guilty of anything; I knew!'

'Knew what?' he persisted intensely, hands clenched at his sides.

'Wolf, I went to the flat that night, spoke to Barbara. Not that I really needed to,' she added bitterly. 'The fact that she was waiting for you wearing only a sexy nightgown and robe should have told its own story! Not that it did at first,' she shook her head self-derisively at her naïveté all those years ago. 'Barbara had to spell it out in black and white for me before I realised exactly why she was there! Even then I couldn't take in the fact that the two of you actually intended spending the night together on the very day her husband—your brother!— had been killed.' She swallowed down her nausea at the memory.

'Barbara spelt it out for you...?' Wolf repeated softly.

'Oh, for goodness' sake, Wolf!' Cyn snapped emotionally. 'She told me all about the affair the two of you had been having for years, how Alex had become suspicious, and that's why you became more deeply involved with me than you had your other models.'

'To allay suspicion from Barbara and me,' Wolf said slowly.

'Of course,' Cyn scorned. 'Usually you only slept with your models, but this time you needed a little camouflage for your affair with your brother's wife, and that's why we became engaged. I don't suppose you ever intended marrying me,' she shook her head ruefully at her stupidity in ever thinking it had been anything else. 'No family or close relatives to placate or explain yourself to, just a convenient little orphan you could dispose of once Alex became less suspicious about you and Barbara!'

'You're wrong, Cyn——'

'All that talk about *our* having a traditional wedding,' she continued in a pained voice. 'The "flowing white gown, the cake with little cupids decorating it, a horse and carriage to drive the bride and groom from the church to the wedding reception——"' To her dismay

Cyn could feel the tears starting to clog her throat as she repeated the words Wolf had taunted her with that day they had met again for the first time in seven years at the Harcourts'; he had known exactly what he was saying that day, exactly how to wound her. He hadn't forgotten any of the things she had told him she would like for their wedding!

'My God, I can't believe this!' groaned Wolf, his hand shaking slightly as he pushed his hair back from his face—a face so pale that he looked grey. 'Cyn, I don't care what Barbara told you about that night, or any other night, but I have never made love to her, nor have I ever had the slightest inclination to do so,' he added with distaste. 'She was at my flat that evening because I was at the hospital with my mother; she had a massive stroke when she was told of Alex's death. And Barbara claimed she didn't want to be at her home alone that night, of all nights.' He shook his head a little dazedly. 'I can't believe we were talking about completely different things that night, that none of the last seven years need have happened . . .' He sat down abruptly, as if his legs would no longer hold him.

Now it was Cyn's turn to stare at him, to try to make some sense of all this. His mother had had the massive stroke *that* night? Somehow she had assumed it had happened some time after Alex's death, not on the very day he died. She had had no idea that that was what Wolf meant that day when he told her his mother had 'collapsed'. It helped to explain Wolf's distraction that day; he couldn't have known who to help first, his seriously ill mother, or his brother's widow!

But what of the things Barbara had said that night? Wolf's own admission that he felt guilty about his actions where Alex was concerned; she hadn't imagined that!

'You admitted your guilt, Wolf,' she reminded him firmly, determined not to show any signs of weakness; if she did she would be lost all over again! 'Told me you'd never forget what you'd done to Alex.'

'But I didn't mean *Barbara*!' he protested strongly, standing up again now and moving across the room towards her. 'It should have been *me* in that helicopter, Cyn. *Me* that died!'

She frowned up at him, searching the hard, contorted planes of his face; she didn't understand.

Wolf grasped her shoulders, his fingers digging painfully into her flesh as he shook her slightly. 'I should have been the one making that business trip, Cyn,' he groaned heavily.

'But——'

'*I* was the elder son, Cyn,' he shook her again. 'Don't you understand?'

And suddenly she did. She had always assumed Alex was the elder, that Wolf, as the younger son, had been allowed to pursue the career he chose. But if Wolf had been the elder, the one expected to take over Thornton Industries on the death of their father, but he had refused to do so because he wanted to paint, then Alex would have been left with no choice but to step into the shoes Wolf had rejected!

She shook her head, tears blurring her vision again. But this time her tears were for Wolf, for the guilt he had known the last seven years because he felt he should have been the one going on that business trip, the one to die, not Alex. 'You're so wrong, Wolf,' she told him in a pained voice. 'Alex enjoyed being head of Thornton Industries. He would have still been in the company even if you *had* been willing to take over when your father died. Alex was a businessman through and through, he enjoyed every aspect of it,' she said without a single doubt. 'Wolf, I honestly believe that whether you were in the company or out of it, it would have made no difference. I believe that when it's your time to die then it happens, whether in a plane crash, a car accident, or simply natural causes. Seven years ago was Alex's time to die, Wolf,' she told him with certainty. 'And nothing you could have said, or done, would have made the slightest difference to that.'

He closed his eyes, swaying slightly. 'Why couldn't you have said all those things to me seven years ago?' he groaned weakly, looking down at her again now. 'Why?'

Because seven years ago she had believed what Barbara told her! She didn't believe her any longer, she was sure now that the affair was wishful thinking on the part of the other woman, that she had played on Cyn's own lack of confidence, her insecurities about a man like Wolf possibly being able to love someone like her. She didn't have those same insecurities now, but, as Wolf said, it was seven years too late . . . !

She looked at him with darkly pained eyes. 'You'll never know how much I wish I had,' she choked. 'Oh, Wolf, what fools we both were!' Because she wasn't the only one to blame. Wolf had to take some of the responsibility for that; his self-recriminations about Alex were totally unnecessary.

His hands gripped her shoulders less tightly now, becoming almost gentle, the thumbs slowly caressing. 'Is it too late, Cyn?' he asked, his gaze intent. 'Too late to turn the clock back and start again?'

Her mouth felt suddenly dry, her eyes wide as she stared up at him. He couldn't mean——! 'Wolf?' was all she could manage to choke out.

His gaze was warm on her face now, the harshness fading from his own face, to be replaced by—— What? Cyn hardly dared to hope!

'I've never stopped loving you, Cyn. Not for a single moment,' he told her huskily, that love shining out of his eyes now. 'When I saw you again at Gerald's house that day I could hardly believe it.' He shook his head. 'I took any opportunity I could to see you again. There was no way I was going to leave your cottage the day I injured my ankle,' he remembered self-mockingly. 'It was just the excuse I needed to be able to spend some time with you, to see if things really were over between us. Just as Rebecca saying you'd talked about me over lunch today was the only excuse I needed to come here tonight to see you.'

Cyn swallowed hard, hardly daring to believe...! 'I've never stopped loving you either,' she told him with a sob, not waiting for him to take her in his arms but launching herself at him, longing for his closeness, his strength, his love!

His mouth claimed hers, their kisses fevered and fierce, as if they would make up for all the time they had lost in those first ecstatic moments of knowing they still loved each other.

Wolf's forehead was slightly damp on hers when he at last looked down at her, their breathing ragged. 'Marry me, Cyn,' he encouraged gruffly. 'Make me sane again.'

'I would be *insane* not to,' she told him breathlessly, still clinging to the broad strength of his shoulders, her body moulded against his; she never wanted to be parted from him again, needed his physical closeness at this moment to reassure her they were finally going to be together. She had a feeling she would feel this way for a long time to come!

He gave a shout of triumph before sweeping her up into his arms and carrying her over to the sofa, sitting down with her on his knee, proceeding to kiss her all over again, their sighs and cries of pleasure the only sound in the cottage for a long time after that.

'Does this mean we're engaged again?' Cyn finally looked up at him teasingly, cradled in his arms as they both lay naked on the sofa; it was hardly strong enough to take their weight, but that hadn't bothered either of them as they showed each other the strength of their love.

'No, it does not,' Wolf said firmly, his tone brooking no argument. 'I've had it with engagements. This time I'm not giving you a chance to change your mind; we're going straight on to the marriage!'

Her fingers traced the tiny damp swirls of hair on his chest. 'Rebecca said you only wanted to get married to provide a Thornton heir,' she said teasingly, but her gaze was curiously intent on the relaxed beauty of his face from their lovemaking.

'I'm not proud of the fact, but in Rebecca's case, yes, that was true,' he admitted ruefully. 'As far as *we're* concerned, I only want you. I don't care if we never have children.'

Cyn gave a rueful smile. 'It's a little late for that, I'm afraid.'

Wolf looked down at her frowningly, his eyes widening at the message he read in her eyes, his mouth opening as if he would speak, and then closing again as he found he couldn't talk, his gaze moving down the silken length of her body to rest on the gentle curve of her stomach.

'Yes, Wolf,' she said almost shyly, taking one of his hands and resting it against her. 'I'm carrying our child in there.' She still looked a little anxious, not completely sure what his reaction was going to be to learning he was going to be a father in eight months' time; after all, he couldn't have got used to the idea that they were getting married yet, let alone take in being a prospective father at the same time!

Cyn had been more than a little taken aback at the realisation of her pregnancy herself, had thought at first that her body was just playing tricks on her, that it was the strain of the last few weeks that had caused her ir-regularity. But as the days passed, and still nothing hap-pened, she had bought herself one of those test-it-at-home-yourself pregnancy kits, and her initial reaction to its being positive was one of sheer disbelief. She couldn't be pregnant from that one time with Wolf! And then she had berated herself for her naïveté; of course she could be pregnant, one time was all it took!

It was because she was pregnant that she had known she couldn't be involved with Rebecca's wedding in August, not even in an advisory capacity. She would be showing by then, and if Wolf should learn of her preg-nancy he was sure to realise he was the father!

How did he feel about it now that she had told him?

He was still looking down at her body, sitting up now, bending down to gently place a kiss where he knew his child nestled inside its mother.

His gaze was dark with emotion as he raised his head to look down at her. 'I'm not going to ask if you would ever have told me if I hadn't come here today and told you I've never stopped loving you,' he assured her huskily. 'It's enough that our child is going to be born into a home where it knows its parents love it, and each other, more than anything else in this world. And that *is* the way I love you, Cyn.' The lean strength of his hands cradled each side of her face now as he gazed down into her eyes. 'Always. And forever.'

And she would never doubt it again. She knew, with her maturity, that she could deal with any obstruction Claudia or Barbara would care to throw against their happiness. Besides, Claudia might just accept her when she knew there was to be a grandchild... And Barbara was no threat to her, never had been.

'And your painting, Wolf,' Cyn prompted softly. 'Surely you have an assistant you can train up to take care of Thorntons while you do what you really love?'

'I really *love* making love to you,' Wolf told her teasingly as his arms tightened about her once again, his body hardening with desire. 'But I'm sure I'll be able to find a few minutes in each day, in between making love to you, to throw some paint on a canvas!'

He did so much more than 'throw paint on a canvas,' but for the moment Cyn was content. She knew she would get Wolf back painting full-time; she also knew that their child was going to have a very famous artist father one of these days. The sooner the better, as far as she was concerned.

But at the moment he was doing that other thing he did so well, so much so that Cyn found she could hardly think at all, completely giving up any idea of doing so as Wolf began to kiss her breasts.

They could talk later. Much later, she groaned, as Wolf's tongue lovingly lathed the tautness of her nipple even as his body claimed hers. This was what was important, what would always be important; their deep, abiding love for each other...

Hi!

I can't believe that I'm living on Cyprus—home of Aphrodite, the legendary goddess of love—or that I'm suddenly the owner of a five-star hotel.

Nikolaos Konstantin obviously can't quite believe any of it, either!

Love, Emily

MILLION DOLLAR SWEEPSTAKES (III)

No purchase necessary. To enter, follow the directions published. Method of entry may vary. For eligibility, entries must be received no later than March 31, 1996. No liability is assumed for printing errors, lost, late or misdirected entries. Odds of winning are determined by the number of eligible entries distributed and received. Prizewinners will be determined no later than June 30, 1996.

Sweepstakes open to residents of the U.S. (except Puerto Rico), Canada, Europe and Taiwan who are 18 years of age or older. All applicable laws and regulations apply. Sweepstakes offer void wherever prohibited by law. Values of all prizes are in U.S. currency. This sweepstakes is presented by Torstar Corp., its subsidiaries and affiliates, in conjunction with book, merchandise and/or product offerings. For a copy of the Official Rules send a self-addressed, stamped envelope (WA residents need not affix return postage) to: MILLION DOLLAR SWEEPSTAKES (III) Rules, P.O. Box 4573, Blair, NE 68009, USA.

EXTRA BONUS PRIZE DRAWING

No purchase necessary. The Extra Bonus Prize will be awarded in a random drawing to be conducted no later than 5/30/96 from among all entries received. To qualify, entries must be received by 3/31/96 and comply with published directions. Drawing open to residents of the U.S. (except Puerto Rico), Canada, Europe and Taiwan who are 18 years of age or older. All applicable laws and regulations apply; offer void wherever prohibited by law. Odds of winning are dependent upon number of eligibile entries received. Prize is valued in U.S. currency. The offer is presented by Torstar Corp., its subsidiaries and affiliates in conjunction with book, merchandise and/or product offering. For a copy of the Official Rules governing this sweepstakes, send a self-addressed, stamped envelope (WA residents need not affix return postage) to: Extra Bonus Prize Drawing Rules, P.O. Box 4590, Blair, NE 68009, USA.

SWP-H894

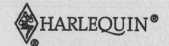

THE WEDDING GAMBLE
Muriel Jensen

Eternity, Massachusetts, was America's wedding town. Paul Bertrand knew this better than anyone—he never should have gotten soused at his friend's rowdy bachelor party. Next morning when he woke up, he found he'd somehow managed to say "I do"—to the woman he'd once jilted! And Christina Bowman had helped launch so many honeymoons, she knew just what to do on theirs!

THE WEDDING GAMBLE, available in September from American Romance, is the fourth book in Harlequin's new cross-line series, **WEDDINGS, INC.**

Be sure to look for the fifth book, **THE VENGEFUL GROOM,** by Sara Wood (Harlequin Presents #1692), coming in October.

WED4

HARLEQUIN®

PRESENTS: *Plus*

Nathan Parnell needs a wife and mother for his young son. Sasha Redford and her daughter need a home. It's a match made in heaven, although no one's discussed the small matter of love.

Emily Musgrave and her nephew are on the run. But has she compounded her problems by accepting the help of Sandy McPherson, a total stranger?

Fall in love with Nathan and Sandy—Sasha and Emily do!

Watch for

In Need of a Wife by Emma Darcy
Harlequin Presents Plus #1679

and

Catch Me If You Can by Anne McAllister
Harlequin Presents Plus #1680

Harlequin Presents Plus
The best has just gotten better!

Available in September wherever Harlequin books are sold.